**Other Lyon and Bea Wentworth
mysteries by Richard Forrest:**

Death Under the Lilacs
The Death at Yew Corner
The Death in the Willows
Death Through the Looking Glass
The Wizard of Death
A Child's Garden of Death

Other novels by Richard Forrest:

The Killing Edge
Who Killed Mr. Garland's Mistress?
Lark

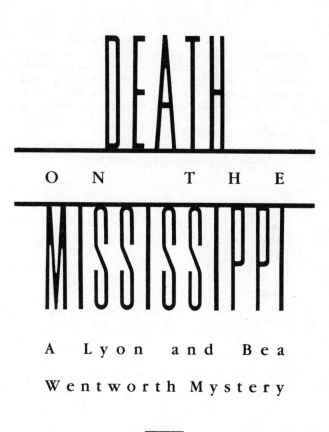

DEATH
ON THE
MISSISSIPPI

A Lyon and Bea
Wentworth Mystery

—

RICHARD FORREST

St. Martin's Press/New York

Design by Judith A. Stagnitto

Library of Congress Cataloging-in-Publication Data

Forrest, Richard
    Death on the Mississippi / Richard Forrest.
      p.   cm.
    ISBN 0-312-03323-0
    I. Title.
    PS3556.0739D48   1989
    813'.54—dc20   89-34858

First Edition

10 9 8 7 6 5 4 3 2 1

For
Phyllis Westberg

DEATH
ON THE
MISSISSIPPI

It would be so easy to destroy them.

A simple mental command could cause a twitch of his right hand on the switch and their existence would end.

Lyon Wentworth was completely disgusted with his Wobblies. He crossed his hands over the word processor and rested his chin on his forearms as he stared out the window at the frolicking pair. His two creations pranced on the stone parapet that separated Nutmeg Hill's patio from the steep drop to the Connecticut River far below.

The Wobblies were performing some sort of ritualistic movement on the narrow ledge. Their tails thumped the stone in time to a silent internal rhythm, and their forked tongues flicked rapidly in and out. They could stray, but it seemed proscribed that they stay within his field of vision. They had been difficult all morning, and now they rejoiced in new-found freedom.

Until they decided to return to the pages of his latest children's book, his literary production for the day would be minimal. It was going to be a long day. He would be forced to remain in his chair, alert before his machine, and hope they would return to remove the ravages of his writer's block.

A new sound from outside was a welcome diversion. He turned to hear the crunch of wheels on gravel in the long drive that led up to the house. He went to open the front door and lean against its frame as two somber vehicles slowed to a careful halt a few feet away. In the lead was a black, four-door sedan whose tinted windows made identification of its occupants impossible. The next in line was a hearse whose driver stared impassively ahead without acknowledging Lyon's presence.

Lyon straightened his lanky frame and walked to the sedan. He was a tall man of asthenic build and sharp features. A shock of blond-browning hair fell in a forelock over his forehead, and it was characteristic for him to sweep it back with his palm as he smiled. He was dressed, as he usually was, in khaki work pants, a loose sport shirt, and topsiders without socks.

The two men who emerged from the black sedan were an unmatched pair dressed in black suits with white shirts and dark ties. At Lyon's right was a squat, heavyset man who clenched a buff-colored file folder. His companion was tall and rangy.

"I am the Reverend Brumby," the squat man said as he extended a limp hand at Lyon. "My associate, Deacon Stockton, will assist me with the services."

"Services?" Lyon glanced nervously at the hearse and

its stoic chauffeur. "You obviously have the wrong house."

Brumby officiously flicked open the folder. "Wentworth, Route Two, Nutmeg Hill, Murphysville, Connecticut."

"Well, yes, that *is* me." The day was deteriorating at a rapid rate. He wondered if it was too early to have a drink. The sun had to be over the yardarm in the Azores.

"Mr. Turman's instructions were quite specific. Surely, his lawyer notified you that the services would be held today?"

Lyon shook his head. "I don't know what in the world you are talking about."

Brumby frowned as he flipped a page in his folder. "You do know the deceased, Dalton Turman?"

"I've known Dalton for years, since we served in the army together."

"And you are aware that his final request was that the services be held at Nutmeg Hill?"

"I didn't even know he had died."

"It was an unfortunate accident at one of his construction sites," Brumby said. "I believe a backhoe ran amok."

"I'm really not prepared . . ." Lyon started to say.

"You need not concern yourself with details, Mr. Wentworth. We are prepared to handle everything." Brumby made a finger signal toward the hearse.

Lyon stepped aside as the three men dressed in black began to efficiently perform their duties. Moving in silent unison, they opened the hearse's rear door, unfolded a gurney, silently slid the coffin from the vehicle onto the rolling stretcher, and pushed it toward the house. They jockeyed the coffin over the doorsill, down the hall into the living room, and immediately began to rearrange furniture.

Within minutes the proper funereal atmosphere had

been achieved. Racks of flowers, brought in from the hearse, were arranged on a portable table behind the coffin. The gurney was draped in black, and the room's remaining furniture had been arranged in rows neatly aligned before the catafalque. Lyon had offered coffee, which had been refused, help, which was also refused; and was now relegated to the role of silent observer standing uselessly by the French doors.

Why had Dalton chosen Nutmeg Hill for his last rites? In the last decade the two men had only met occasionally perhaps once a year. The dead man's reasons were immaterial, for it was an obligation that must be fulfilled. Dalton had saved Lyon's life, and he would forever be indebted.

The Reverend Brumby stepped back from the coffin and quietly surveyed the room. He seemed satisfied, and nodded at Deacon Stockton, who returned to the car. "The services will be at two, Mr. Wentworth."

"Will there be anyone else here?"

"I believe there are a few select invited guests."

"I see," Lyon replied. He wondered, considering the seemingly shoddy efficiency of Dalton's executor's, whether anyone else would arrive. Brumby was unscrewing the coffin's lid. "What are you doing?" Lyon asked in alarm.

"Mr. Turman's last instructions specifically ordered an open-coffin service."

"Open coffin?" Lyon feared a horrific vision of Dalton's mutilated corpse as it might appear after having been crushed by a backhoe. He averted his head as the coffin lid was slowly raised.

Brumby folded his hands reverently. "So lifelike, so natural. Don't you think so, Mr. Wentworth?"

Lyon stood at the foot of the casket and looked down at the corpse. The rows of banked flowers to the rear were

4

beginning to cast a sickening sweetish odor in the room. The pleated fabric lining the casket's interior appeared cheap and hastily installed. Dalton would never have approved. The dead man's face was hardly lifelike. It was chalk white, the features so alabaster they resembled a death mask. Dalton did not look asleep. As with most of the dead, he appeared dead.

Deacon Stockton returned to the house carrying a large wicker basket. "Where do we put the snakes?"

"The what?" Lyon whirled in astonishment to look at the large wicker basket. It began to sway in Stockton's grasp as living things inside shifted position.

"These are the snakes we handle during the service. We do a great snake routine, and if things really go right, people will speak in tongues."

"And ye shall handle serpents, and they shall not smite thee of true faith," Brumby intoned.

Stockton removed the cover of the basket. "Want to see?" He lifted a large timber rattlesnake whose tail immediately coiled over his arm. "George here has some great moves. He's a real crowd pleaser."

"We also brought a copperhead that's not exactly stage shy," Brumby added.

Stockton reluctantly stuffed the snake back into the basket. "Got a safe place for them, Wentworth? We don't like to leave them near the coffin during the viewing. Sometimes the bereaved accidentally kick over the basket, and then there's hell to pay."

"I'll find a place," Lyon said as he carried the basket into the kitchen. As he searched the room for a safe location, he wondered how speaking in tongues and the handling of serpents were going to strike a taciturn New England audience. He found a secure place in a lower dish cabinet large enough for the basket, and returned to the living room. He'd have to warn Rocco about the snakes so that the gargantuan police officer could stand at the rear of the room during that part of the service. Rocco might be nearly fearless in almost all situations, but his friend had one strong aversion, the object of which now rested in the kitchen.

He walked over to the coffin to look down at the dead Dalton Turman. "At least you're consistent to the end," Lyon said aloud.

The corpse's eyes snapped open as the body rose in the coffin. "Prankenstein strikes again!" Dalton Turman said before breaking into a high falsetto laugh.

The Governor of the State of Connecticut fought to control his rage as he confronted Senator Bea Wentworth.

The Governor was convinced that he was not a complete antifeminist. In fact, as he often told himself, he was married to a woman. A couple of his children were female. His Lieutenant Governor and one of his predecessors had been of the opposite gender, and there was a young lady in Winstead who . . . but, to be opposed in fiscal matters dear to his political future by his own Senate Majority Leader, a member of his own party and . . . He clenched his jaw to stifle a sexist epithet.

Outside of reaching for the thirty-eight police special clamped to the inside of the desk well and shooting his Majority Leader, there was only one course of action. It was pipe-tamping time. He reached for the tobacco humidor and began to methodically stuff his pipe with fresh mixture. He tamped the bowl gently with a sterling silver pestle and peered thoughtfully through horn-rims at Bea Wentworth. The Governor was not particularly fond of pipes, he preferred Cuban cigars, and his eyesight was perfect; but both props added to the thoughtful image he had cultivated over the years. The methodical and plodding routine was working. Bea was on the edge of her seat, her body tense as she leaned toward him.

"Tell me, Senator, do you really think it is appropriate to tack a children's day-care—center amendment to our general revenue bill?"

"You want budget approval and I want day care," Bea said. "That's the way it's going to be."

"The opposition just might blow us out of the water on this one, Senator," the Governor said mildly. He was proud of his self-control. It had taken years to curb his natural inclination to pound desks.

"I think I have most of the votes necessary, and it's so close to the end of the session that I can use some Senators' natural impatience as leverage." She stood at his desk with both hands curled over its edge. "With your help, we can pull this off, Governor."

"Without your costly amendment we would have a cozy surplus that we could use in other ways." Day care for welfare mothers amounted to zilch votes, he thought to himself. A cut in the capital-gains tax would bring in big bucks at the next campaign-contribution solicitation. If only he could find some old-fashioned dirt on this broad he might be able to control his Majority Leader. It wasn't from lack of trying. Last year he'd sent two members of his "confidential team" to Murphysville, where Wentworth lived. They had been instructed to dig around in the Senator's life and also look into the background of that nerd husband of hers. They had discovered zip, and after a couple of days the local police chief got on their case and threw them out of town.

It was pipe-lighting time, and that always took awhile. As the Governor worked on an even light, he observed the woman sitting across from him. Bea was not a large woman, but her compact figure was too full for her to be called petite. Her close-cropped, light hair often gave her a gamine-like appearance, an impression that could be quickly dispelled by watching her darting, intelligent eyes and an intense manner that revealed itself when she was concerned. She was concerned now.

Didn't this woman ever get drunk and do dumb things? Didn't she ever play around? Maybe her husband liked boys, that used to be good for a little political extortion.

He glanced at the blinking light on his call director and impatiently snatched the phone. "What?" He reluctantly handed the phone to Bea. "It's your office."

"Your husband called and said it was important for you to know that Dalton has arrived," the efficient voice said.

For a few moments the Governor of the State of Connecticut thought he had found deliverance. His Senate Majority Leader had turned pale, the hand clasping the phone shook, and she sat limply in the chair. She gave every appearance of having just suffered a minor stroke.

Bea shucked off a light suit jacket and threw her key ring on the hall table. She sighed. It had not been one of her better days. "I'm home!"

"Out on the patio," Lyon answered.

The soothing ambiance of Nutmeg Hill embraced and rejuvenated her as she walked past Lyon's study to the living room. They had discovered the two-hundred-year-old house with its gambrel roof and widow's walk on a long-ago Sunday hike. Boarded up and half hidden by plant growth, they had sensed that once it was refurbished the house on its spectacular perch on a promontory above the Connecticut River would fulfill all their expectations. It had taken years of hard work, but now that it was completed, their dream had come to fruition.

Her restored mood shattered when she saw the coffin in the living room.

She wouldn't ask. It wasn't necessary to know details now that Dalton Turman was back in town.

She mixed a martini for herself and poured a pony of

Dry Sack sherry for Lyon at the bar cart and took the drinks out on the patio. Next to the parapet wall, Lyon was adjusting the tripod of his telescope. "Are we bird watching or is Debbi Wilcox skinny dipping off her dock again?" she asked as she put his sherry down on the wall.

Lyon shook his head as he glanced through the eyepiece. "You've got to see Dalton's latest acquisition."

"I will not look at his newest toy," Bea said. "I will not even acknowledge his existence."

Lyon made a minute adjustment to the telescope's lens. "I've never seen anything like this. Dalton had it designed and built to his own specifications, and he plans to sail it down the Inland Waterway to Florida."

"I refuse to look," Bea said. "You know, of course, that a practical joker of modest means is limited to exploding cigars and whoopee cushions. A rich practical joker is a menace to humanity, in the same category as depletion of the ozone layer and the sales tax."

"I take it we had a bad day in the Senate?"

"It wasn't exactly the ides of March, but if this state had a Tower of London, our commander in chief would have me billeted there."

"I knew you were going to have trouble with that rider to the revenue bill."

"I expected objections from fearless leader, and I think I can handle it. But, one thing I can not cope with tonight is making dinner for that man."

"And his new wife."

"The poor girl. The possible events on their wedding night boggles the mind."

Lyon laughed. "Dalton expected that reaction, so it's his treat. The caterers arrive at six, a few guests at seven. Come on now, take a look at this thing."

"I guess I'll have to." She bent over to peer through the telescope as Lyon went for fresh drinks.

The houseboat was temporarily berthed at a rickety wooden pier in a wooded cove on the far side of the Connecticut River. She estimated it to be seventy or eighty feet in length with rectangular lines. There was a ladder and swimming platform at the stern, a canopied rear deck, a main saloon with many windows, and a large foreward area for staterooms. The bow's slight curve gave the craft its only semblance of streamlining. A tall superstructure contained a wide pilot house and high mast that bristled with various types of radio dishes and antennas. Mahogany and teakwood rails with brass fittings shined in the dying sunlight.

She sensed Lyon back at her side. "It looks like Tara on pontoons."

"He never does anything halfway."

"If this telescope were attached to a cannon I could blow it out of the water."

"Such sentiments from the state's leading proponent of strict gun-control legislation?"

"That's rifles and handguns. I'm talking howitzers and missiles."

"Did you notice the boat's name? The *Mississippi*."

"Bring your drink and talk to me while I shower."

Bea let the multiple shower sprays tingle her body with water as warm as she could tolerate. She turned slowly from right to left as the water massaged away the day's tension. She had left the translucent shower door cracked and could see half of Lyon through the opening.

"You know, Wentworth," she said over the sound of running water. "I'm going to have the state librarian research the last witch burning we had in the town of Murphysville."

"Don't be sexist. It was a warlock in sixteen forty-five."

"It's my thought that it wasn't a witch . . . warlock at all, but some guy who pulled a massive trick on the town that made them all so mad that they did him in. The burning stake was probably too good for him."

"You're too hard on Dalton, hon. I don't think I ever told you this, but he saved my life in combat."

Bea sighed.

"I was ordered by the regimental commander to occupy an FO position in front of our lines," Lyon continued. "The gooks had evidently infiltrated a mortar team to my right."

"Damn it, Lyon! Don't say gooks."

"The enemy aggressors, then. Anyway, I was observing a suspicious wooded draw to my front when all hell broke loose."

"Trapped, unable to break free, I was going to be overrun," Bea mumbled as she turned her face directly up toward the overhead spray.

"Trapped, unable to break free, I was going to be overrun," Lyon said.

"At great personal risk, Lieutenant Turman and a squad of men fought their way to my position," Bea said softly.

"Putting his life in jeopardy, Lieutenant Turman and a few guys fought their way to me," Lyon said.

"We've been married too long," Bea yelled at him.

The shower door opened as Lyon stepped inside. Somehow, during his war story he had undressed. He began to knead the tense muscles in Bea's neck. "We haven't been married that long," he said.

"I love late-afternoon matinees," Bea said as she turned to press against him.

2 André, the caterer, wore tight dress pants, a black turtleneck sweater, and should have carried a swagger stick. He directed his staff with expansive, nearly soundless commands, and obviously expected immediate obedience and efficiency. He barely paused before the coffin as he closed the lid and nodded for a tablecloth to be spread across its top.

"I assume we serve the buffet from here?" he asked Lyon with a wave at the casket.

"Oh, yes," Lyon replied. "It's only used during daylight hours."

André gave a barely perceptible shrug and continued his supervision of the preparations on the patio.

"This proves that we've been going to the wrong parties for years," Bea said.

"I don't think it would have bothered André if the casket held Quasimodo clutching a gargoyle." For a few moments they silently observed the preparations. "And to think that we thought cold cuts and a loaf of rye bread constituted a buffet," Lyon observed.

"How gauche we've been," Bea said as she sniffed the aroma of Persian chicken as it was delicately removed from warming containers and placed in silver chafing dishes. The other courses were of equal quality: iced melon, steamed white rice, vegetables en brochette, and peaches sultana. She could not tell if the wide bottles of Meursault nestling in their wine buckets were medium-priced or expensive. She doubted they were a bad year.

They went out onto the patio as André lit the Japanese lanterns that had been strung along the parapet. A formal bar, manned by a white-jacketed waiter, had been erected near the far wall.

Guests swirled into the house cloaked in an envelope of laughter. They seeped into the living room and spilled out the French doors to the patio. One intense couple invaded Lyon's study where they held an intimate conversation that immediately ceased whenever anyone approached.

Lyon realized that outside of Bea and Dalton, the only person he recognized was his friend, the police chief, Rocco Herbert.

An admiring entourage surrounded Dalton as he completed a story. "His face! God, you should have seen Wentworth's face when I winked at him from my funeral bier."

"You're incorrigible," someone in the entourage said.

"Of course I am," Dalton said as he grasped Bea and

pulled her into his arms for a hearty buss. "Madam Senator."

Dalton smiled at her. He had a wide, crooked smile that seemed to wander over his elongated face. He was an extremely tall man with pinched facial features that were dominated by a longish nose and deep-set eyes that appeared slightly too small for his large head. His body was rangy and gave his physical movements a sectionalized appearance as he walked.

He lifted Bea by the waist and set her on the parapet wall. "Ladies and gentlemen, our hostess. Beatrice Wentworth, Senator of all she surveys. When I came to build in Connecticut, I looked up my old army buddy, Lyon, and asked for his political recommendation because every developer needs a foot in the state house, right! Well, Old Lyon told me about this politician that he was in bed with, and what's good enough for Lyon is good enough for me. Bea is not only pretty, but she doesn't come cheap. She costs me a bundle, but I believe in the best legislators money can buy."

Rocco Herbert lounged against the French doors that led to the patio. Lyon handed the police chief a brandy snifter of pepper vodka. The gargantuan police officer scowled at Dalton. "Someone is going to kill that guy one day."

"I have it on good authority that it takes a silver bullet."

"How can you allow him to ridicule Bea that way?"

"No one takes what he says seriously."

"You're going to regret that loyalty someday, Lyon. That little favor he did for you in Asia was years ago, and that was what he was supposed to do anyway, goddamn it!"

"I'm here tonight because of him."

Dalton stood on a chair and swiveled one of the yard spotlights until its beam bracketed Lyon. "And over there," he said to the crowd from his perch on the chair, "is our cohost, famed porno writer, Lyon Wentworth."

Lyon laughed and Rocco growled into his brandy snifter. "I write children's books," Lyon yelled back at Dalton.

"Do you hear that, folks? He makes up kiddie porn, the real dregs. What a great guy!"

The party continued. Some guests wandered into the living room to sample the buffet, while others, the serious drinkers, seemed tethered to locations near the patio bar. Babel and noise overwhelmed Lyon until he was unable to differentiate individual sentences, phrases, or even words. Each voice seemed to speak in at least one register above normal, and it all merged into a sea of cacophony. He tuned out.

Rocco found him in the darkest corner of the patio wedged into a corner where the parapet met the house wall. "Are you blotto or hiding?"

"Definitely the latter and working on the former."

Rocco handed him a fresh pony of Dry Sack sherry and pulled on his own voluminous vodka. "You know, Lyon, now that Dalton is back on our case, it makes me next on his list. It's not a question of if I'm going to get it, it's a question of *when* I'm going to get it."

Dalton steered Bea and a woman with cascading blond hair across the patio toward them. "Well, Pan, you've met Lyon and Bea. The large monster here is called a Rocco."

Rocco took her hand. "We commiserate with your recent misfortune."

"Something I don't know about?" she said in a puzzled voice with a strong Southern accent.

"Marrying Dalton is absolute disaster," Rocco said.

"Pandora was voted Miss Conviviality in the Miss America Pageant," Dalton said. "That was my immediate attraction. I had always wondered what happened to such gushingly sweet girls."

"They become airline stewardesses like I did," Pan said.

"Where I discovered her," Dalton said. "High over the Mississippi Delta as she twitched down the aisle to bring my bourbon."

"Thus the name of your boat," Lyon said.

"Actually, Mississippi is where Pan's cousins intermarry and multiply in great numbers."

"Most of them wore shoes to the wedding, darling."

"Do you ever say anything nice about anyone, Dalton?" Bea asked.

"Not if it's avoidable."

"If I don't divorce him, I'm going to kill him," Pandora said as she grasped her husband's arm affectionately.

"Now there's the soul of a true Miss Conviviality," Dalton said. "She gives me a choice."

"After a few weeks living with you, darling," Pan said, "Mother Theresa would become a terrorist."

An extremely tall woman with a fully proportioned figure crossed the patio to them and put her arm over Dalton's shoulder. "Does our verbal venom have its usual tangy taste?"

Dalton's smile was diabolical. "Ah, Katrina, you must meet my old and dear friends." He made the introductions. "And people, this is Katrina Loops, often known as the 'Hartford Humper.' I won't describe exactly what she does, but suffice to say that when a telephone rings she begins to take off her clothes."

Katrina smiled at him. "Only for French phones, darling."

Lyon felt Bea plucking at his sleeve. He caught her eye and they retreated into the relative quiet of the kitchen.

"That Loops woman is really something," Lyon said. "She's a very, very large lady."

Bea's look not only told him that she knew what he was thinking, but that he knew that she knew. "Don't even think about it, Wentworth," she said. "Don't even consider it in your wildest fantasies."

"She's so big, and each part is so perfectly fashioned."

"I'll gain weight if that's your bag."

"You'd also need over a foot in height."

"My enthusiasm makes up for what I lack in stature."

Rocco stuck his head into the kitchen. "Phone for you, Bea. It's the Governor."

"Tell the Governor that I'll call him back as soon as my cell meeting is over."

"Are you sure you want me to say that?" Rocco asked.

"How about we're having a swingers party and I'm presently encumbered with three motorcycle guys."

Rocco frowned. "I know the Governor's voice."

"It's really him?"

"Really."

"I'll use the phone in your study, Lyon," Bea said as she hurried from the room. "That is if that couple in there are not yet obscenely occupied."

When Lyon was alone in the kitchen he began looking for an additional bottle of sherry. He opened a lower kitchen cabinet and quickly snapped it shut. The sound evidently awakened the snakes and caused them to stir so that the basket thumped against surrounding glassware. He made a mental note to ask Dalton to make snake-removal arrangements before the evening was over. He found the sherry in a high cabinet over the sink and was uncorking it when she spoke from behind him.

"Mr. Wentworth . . . ah, Lyon."

He turned to see Pandora Turman standing stiffly by the refrigerator. Her blue eyes, deeply shaded with makeup, squinted as she looked at him intently. He wondered if her intensity was due to astigmatism or emotion.

"Can I get you something, Pan? I was just opening some sherry."

"A bourbon and Coke would be great."

Her words were truncated and fired in a rapid burst composed of a Southern accent mixed with nervous tension. He reached for the bourbon as she watched his movements carefully. His male antennae were not receiving. He wondered why the statuesque Katrina Loops could send him strong sexual signals while this obviously attractive woman seemed nearly asexual. Perhaps it was because she was the cheerleader type, the proverbial girl-next-door—so wholesome and sister-image provoking that lust became nearly incestuous.

He handed her the drink and she took a hefty swig. "I'm sorry we missed the wedding," Lyon said, "but we just weren't able to get to Jackson on two days' notice. As I recall, I think Bea had an important vote in the senate and . . ."

"That's all right," she answered. It came out sounding remarkably like "salright." "You know Dalton. He's always on a spur-of-the-moment calendar. We woke up one morning and he said it was Tuesday, which it was, and that was probably as good a day as any to marry, but it turned out that it had to be on Thursday for complicated reasons. Believe me, it's hard for a girl to get ready and marry on two days' notice. Dalton said there were tax advantages if we did it before the first of the year."

Lyon laughed. "That's as good a reason as any." He knew of one mutual friend who married her long-time lover in order to cover him on her health insurance.

"Dalton says that you're his best friend," she said as her hand brushed his sleeve as if asking for physical confirmation of the statement.

He felt vaguely embarrassed and tried to avoid eye contact for he detected a note of pleading in the remark. "We manage to see each other a time or two a year."

"Then you two are close?" she pressed.

"Let's say that I owe him."

The answer seemed to satisfy her. "Then his jokes don't really bother you?"

"If you're going to be around him you have to tolerate it."

"Has he told you about the threatening calls?"

"Telephone calls?"

"They seem to come at all hours of the night. In the beginning Dalton tried to hide them from me. He'd either go into another room to take the call, or tell whoever it was that he'd call back. But the other night I got on the extension and heard what was said."

"You might have misunderstood the conversation."

"I tried to convince myself of that too, but then the accidents began to happen. A backhoe slid down an embankment, and if Dalton hadn't been able to jump into a nearby ditch, he would have been killed. Two days ago the brakes on the car just went. I was with him when it happened. We were both almost killed when he lost control and we went off the road into some high bushes."

Lyon was having difficulty following her rapid-fire speech and the abrupt shifts in content. Pandora was afflicted with the same problem as others he knew. They assumed that you were aware of most things that transpired in their lives and could therefore initiate conversations in mid-thought. "Hold on a sec. Let's go back to the phone calls. What was said that made you think it was a threat?"

"It was the whole conversation. Like the guy would say things like, 'It's over, Dalton. You've had it this time. You either come across or we get serious.' Sometimes Dalton hangs up, but they call right back and I try to listen in."

"It's always a male voice?" Lyon wondered if the night calls could all be accounted for by a love triangle.

"I thought about women before I listened in. I mean,

before Dalton and I got together he wasn't exactly a priest. But it's always the same voice. A deep, gravellike voice."

"There could be perfectly reasonable explanations for the calls," Lyon said. "After all, Dalton is a developer, and builders deal with a lot of men who didn't go to finishing school."

"What about the accidents? We came within feet of getting killed in the car." Her voice had risen to panic level.

"It was inches, my dear. Unquestionably centimeters, and perhaps even microns." Dalton's high laugh punctuated his arrival in the kitchen. He put a protective arm around his wife. "Baby doll, if I cried every time I was in a near-accident I wouldn't be able to build a small doghouse."

"I still think you should talk to Lyon about it. He's used to getting involved in things like this."

"You have it turned around, orange blossom. *I* am the savior and Lyon is the savee." He clapped Lyon on the shoulder. "Can you imagine this klutz trying to protect me on a construction site?"

"Is there anything to all this?" Lyon asked.

"Wanting to remove me with extreme prejudice? Sure, and it's a long list. I run a nonunion job and a few days ago I threw a union organizer off the property. That's about as smart as volunteering for Masada to complete your retirement time in the Jewish Legion. Then there are the idiots I bought the last piece of property from. They're crying that I took advantage of them now that they suspect what my bottom line is going to be when the job is completed. Finally, there's the people I pull pranks on, and that's a really long list."

"You're not treating this seriously," Pan said as she tore away from her husband's encircling grip. "If I'm going to be a widow, at least do the decent thing and make me a rich one."

"Pandy baby, go circulate and see if any of the guests need coffee, tea, or their pillows fluffed."

"Drop dead, duck butter." She stiff-armed the swinging door as she left.

"She's right, isn't she?" Lyon said.

Dalton smiled crookedly. "Hell, yes. I'm in deep shit with a certain group. If things don't work out I'll be lucky to get off with a couple busted kneecaps."

"That sounds like you're doing business with two-legged banking facilities."

"God, Went! You're an incurable snoop. Let's just say that I take what I consider to be acceptable business risks. Okay? Let's leave it at that."

Bea and Rocco burst into the kitchen. "All right, you guys. The party needs you. In other words, out!"

"What did the Governor allow?" Lyon asked.

"If I drop my day-care ammendment he will ask me to run as Lieutenant Governor."

"Last I heard, Maggie held that job," Lyon retorted.

"Fearless leader has dirt on Maggie. It seems she smoked a joint in nineteen seventy-eight."

"That's despicable," Lyon said. "Of course you have a duty to the people."

"I'm going to seriously consider it after I have a hit. Anyone got any?"

"Don't look at me," Rocco said. "I don't even confiscate single joints from the kids anymore."

"I can't wait until his next offer," Bea said with a laugh.

The tempo of the party had increased with the intro-duction of a combo that had miraculously appeared and started playing in a corner of the patio. Rocco resumed his stance by the French doors as he watched the dancers with a bemused smile on his face. Lyon stood next to his friend. Their disparity in size set them apart, as did their personalities: Lyon's fey, bookish approach to life, and

Rocco's law enforcement career, which sometimes placed the large officer in violent confrontations. And yet over the years their friendship had grown, each man attracted to the other by the very characteristics that set them apart.

"If this party gets any noisier, the neighbors are going to complain," Rocco said.

"You know damn well there isn't a neighbor within a thousand yards of here."

Rocco gave his usual half-smile. "Maybe a cop will call the cops. You got any more pepper vodka left?"

"There's some in the lower kitchen cabinet."

Rocco went through the swinging door. Lyon sipped on his sherry until his friend's bass voice thundered from the kitchen loudly enough to immediately silence the party.

"Snakes!" Rocco boomed. "They *are* snakes!"

Lyon dropped his snifter and spilled sherry across the carpet as he bolted for the kitchen. "Not your gun," he said aloud as he pushed at the swinging door. "Please not the gun."

The first shot from the .357 Magnum reverberated through the house and echoed from the surrounding hills. It was quickly followed by several other shots in rapid-fire sequence.

In midmorning sunlight, Bea Wentworth lightly ran her fingers along a teakwood rail on the houseboat's starboard side. "This is what Noah could have done with the ark if he'd had the money," she said.

They had spent the last hour touring the *Mississippi* with an exuberant Dalton as their guide. Lyon was impressed, and even Bea, whose admiration of Dalton was far from gigantic, had seemed a little awed at the lavish accoutrements.

They had begun with the pilot house ("bridge" in Dalton's nomenclature) located above the saloon. The state-of-the-art electronic equipment would have rivaled the fire-control center on the aircraft carrier *Enterprise*. They had been lectured on each instrument's capabilities and functions, but to Lyon the descriptions had merged into a mass of amperage, bytes, and K memories. The final result of all the gadgetry seemed to be to allow someone to steer downstream. Lyon recalled that Mark Twain's river pilots performed these same duties on the Mississippi with far less equipment.

Bristling antennas and radar discs on the high mast aided the bridge instruments or else allowed Dalton to receive direct television reception from Bulgaria.

Living accommodations on the boat were spacious and lavishly decorated. The main saloon had a three-sided panoramic view of the water through large floor-to-ceiling windows. Privacy was assured by remote-controlled drapes that slid soundlessly across the windows at a touch of a button. Behind the saloon was a formal dining room and a compact but fully equipped galley. Four staterooms, each with private bath, completed the living quarters.

As they toured through the houseboat, Bea would occasionally turn to Lyon and purse her lips. He knew that her staunch New England heritage rebelled at this surfeit of ostentation.

"Brunch on the poop deck, everyone," Pandora said with a wave toward the stern. "Or whatever that place back there is called."

A buffet had been laid out under the awning, and Bobby Douglas, the ship's professional mate, was preparing Bloody Marys at a small bar.

Dalton steered Lyon to the bar. "Bobby's Bloodys will either kill you or cure you. Either way, they may blow the top of your head off." He handed Lyon a tall frosted glass.

Lyon sipped the drink. "Strong, very strong, but good."

"Douglas has done it again. Our mate was one of Flor-

ida's best drug runners until he took a bullet in the leg fired by an angry Colombian."

Lyon judged the mate to be on the good side of thirty. He had sun-bleached brown hair that had turned nearly blond. His tan was of the deep variety that wouldn't fade in the darkest of winters. He wore starched white duck pants, and a T-shirt that revealed firm biceps. The only fault in his near-perfect physique was a slight limp.

"Let's take her downstream and over to the job, Bobby," Dalton said as they joined Bea and Pandora at a table. Bobby Douglas nodded, set a pitcher of Bloody Marys on the table, and climbed a ladder to the saloon roof. In minutes they were heading slowly down the Connecticut River toward Long Island Sound.

Dalton took a large sip from his drink. "I am going to show you the newest down-and-dirty deal, which is also going to make us one hell of a lot of money."

Bea arched an eyebrow. "Legally?"

Dalton smiled. "But of course. It has to do with a magnificent joke called time sharing. We're completely refurbishing the old Pincus resort, all the rooms, cottages, and recreational facilities. When finished we shall convert to condominiums and sell time shares."

"That's not unusual," Lyon said. "Where's the joke?"

"Dwell on these figures a moment. If I remodel one of the waterside cottages with common interest in the other facilities, I can sell it for maybe two hundred thou, right?"

"That seems to be about market around here," Lyon said.

"Now, instead of selling the cottage to one owner, we're going to sell weekly shares at ten thousand per. If my math is correct, that comes to roughly half a mil or more than double what I can get from a single-owner sale. It's capitalism at its best," Dalton said as he raised the pitcher of drinks to pour.

Lyon's world exploded in a film of red.

"Incoming!" was Dalton's hoarse yell.

Although it had been years since he had heard the word, Lyon reacted instinctively. He catapulted himself out of his chair and across the table, while his right arm grasped Bea's shoulder and pulled her forward and under him. They tumbled into a heap on the deck. He scrabbled forward, clutching Bea as he sought the protection of the deck housing.

The shot sound echoed across the water.

Bea's face was bathed in red. He frantically ran his fingers across her cheeks and back into her hairline searching for the wound.

Her tongue flicked across her lips. "Bloody Marys," she said. "And you're wearing them too."

The shadow of Bobby Douglas fell across their bodies as he hunched over at the top of the ladder that led to the deck house roof. He leaped, landed on the balls of his feet, and quickly rolled over to the protection of the rail. He held an automatic handgun in each fist and tossed one across the deck to Dalton, who deftly caught it.

"Not funny, guys," Bea said.

"Did you see a muzzle flash?" Dalton asked Bobby as he ignored Bea's remark.

"Not a thing. I was watching the channel markers."

"Just the one shot that shattered the pitcher," Dalton said. "We must be out of range, but take us out another thousand yards, Bobby. They won't be able to get us with anything but a cannon."

"Yes, sir." Bobby Douglas ran along the seaward side of the houseboat and climbed back to the pilot house.

Pandora began to whimper in the corner. "They're going to kill us," she choked. "I know they are."

"It was probably some kids plinking in the marsh," Dalton said.

"With a thirty-thirty?" Lyon asked.

"I think he's funning us and it's damn sadistic," Bea said.

Dalton tried to smile. "One of my lesser pranks."

Pan stood, glaring down at her husband. "It's not one of his jokes. They're trying to get him and he won't do anything about it."

"Listen, space bunny," Dalton said as he reached up and grasped her hand and pulled her back to the deck next to him. "They're only trying to scare us."

She buried her head in his shoulder. "Well, they're succeeding."

"Are you going to radio the Coast Guard and State Police?" Lyon asked.

Dalton shook his head. "No way. Questions like that I don't need."

Lyon stood in the pilot house with Bobby Douglas as the mate expertly navigated the cumbersome craft around several small rock islands. He handed Lyon a pair of binoculars. "Off the bow at two o'clock is where the resort property begins."

"Thanks." Lyon adjusted the field on the glasses and swept the shoreline until he focused on a man and woman walking down a broad expanse of lawn to the pier. In the background was a large main building, surrounded by a phalanx of cottages, outbuildings, tennis courts, gardens, and a huge swimming pool. Workmen occupied scaffoldings or operated construction equipment as the task of refurbishing continued. "Who's that?" Lyon gestured toward the two people who now waited expectantly at the edge of the dock.

Douglas throttled back on the engines and began to work the craft toward the pier. "The big guy is Sam Idelweise, the construction foreman. He's the only one around here that does any real work. The Amazon in the bikini is . . ."

"I've met Miss Loops," Lyon said and wished that she hadn't chosen a string bathing suit as greeting attire.

As the houseboat pulled parallel to the pier, but before Dalton had a chance to secure the bow line, Sam Idelweise jumped aboard and began an earnest dialogue with him.

"Jesus Christ! You'd think Sam could hold his problems until we docked this scow," Douglas said as he killed the engines and limped forward to complete the docking.

"Hi there," Katrina said to Lyon. She reached for his hand as he took the long step to the dock. Bea smiled tightly and climbed ashore unaided.

Dalton shook his head in an obvious end to his conversation with Idelweise and gestured to Lyon to join them. "Wentworths, meet Sam Idelweise. He looks like a drunken longshoreman, but he's actually our construction foreman. Can't build a damn thing, but he can smell a union organizer a mile away."

The large man wearing muddy work boots and dusty pants waved at them.

"Kat," Dalton continued. "Take the Wentworths off and do your thing."

Katrina gestured toward a small cottage at the water's edge. "The bedroom's finished in that one," she said as she took Lyon's hand and led him across the grassy slope toward the building.

"Am I supposed to watch?" Bea asked with an edge to her voice.

"I'd love to have you participate," Katrina said with a laugh. "You might learn something from my technique."

"I truly doubt that there is anything new in that area," Bea said.

Katrina turned from Lyon to look back at Bea. "My

God! I just realized what you're thinking. It never occurred to me that you'd believe Dalton."

"It seemed in character."

"Senator Wentworth, I'm the sales manager for the Pincus Resort. Dalton thought it would be fun if you heard
our sales pitch. When it comes to sex, why, sometimes I
don't even put out on the first date." She hurried ahead of
them toward the cottage.

"Pity," Lyon said.

Bea glared.

Katrina Loops seemed able to slip into her marketing
persona with ease. She took Dalton's command literally
and subjected them to the full sales presentation. Bea,
whose own sense of the dramatic had been honed by
years on the political scene, was able to appreciate the
fine-tuned orchestration the tall Katrina presented. The
sales manager's approach featured a subtle sexuality directed toward Lyon, combined with an inchoate sister-
bonding superiority with Bea. This barely perceptible
sexist approach manipulated the targets (the potential
customer, she informed them in an aside) in such a manner that both male and female responded to the sales
message in different but positive ways.

Bea could not approve of such sexist manipulation, but
realized that it worked. Although she lived in a beautiful
home only a few miles away, she found herself tempted
to sign a contract.

"I'll sign. I'll buy one," Lyon said.

"Wow, you're good at this," Bea had to admit.

"It pays pretty damn well," Katrina said. "I get a nice
commission on each unit I sell personally, and an override on any sold by my sales people. Let me tell you, it
sure beats waiting tables." She glanced at her wristwatch.
"Listen, I have an appointment with a live one in two

29

minutes. We've completed the tour except for the main building. Would you mind awfully if I left you on your own for a while? Dalton says cocktails on the esplanade in an hour."

"We can amuse ourselves," Bea said. "Go right ahead." Hand in hand they ambled along the walkways that wound past gardens and pools. Gas lamps had been installed in strategic positions so that at night their flickering light would cast leaf shadows along the paths. The walks had been constructed in such a way that from any point there was a water view.

They turned a corner to find themselves facing one of the small cottages that was undergoing complete restoration. Three shirtless young men wearing nail aprons were shingling the roof. Sam Idelweise stood on the ground looking up at their progress as he shook his head in disbelief.

"Grip the goddamn hammer by the base of the handle, you cookie cutters," he yelled up to his young crew. "God save me from college kids pretending to be summer carpenters," he said to the Wentworths.

"They look pretty good to me," Bea said. "That one in the middle has great pecs." Idelweise looked puzzled and Lyon looked stricken. "Two can play this game, Wentworth," she said.

"I need to talk." Sam directed them to a bench far enough from the cottage to give them privacy.

"You want to speak to me because I'm Dalton's friend," Lyon said. He was getting used to the role.

"Jesus, yes. You got it right. Dalton said you were quick on the uptake."

"You want to talk about money."

"How does he do that?" Idelweise asked Bea.

"Practice," she replied.

"You've got to get through to that guy and wake the

asshole up. This is one hell of a sweet job, but he's fucking it up."

"Why don't you just leave this flutching job and work some flutching place else?" Bea said sweetly.

"Sorry about my language, Mrs. Wentworth. You get used to talking like that in construction. I can't leave this job. I got a piece of the action and my name is on some of the paper."

"In the event of chapter eleven or worse, they can't pierce the corporate veil to touch your personal assets," Bea said.

"I don't know about any veil crap, but I do know that yours truly and his house and personal bank accounts is on at least two notes that asshole talked me into signing."

"How can they take your house if this is a corporation?" Lyon asked.

"They certainly can if Sam signed personally in addition to signing as a corporate officer," Bea said. "Banks love the additional protection of getting personal notes as guarantees."

"They called it a 'personal inducement success factor.' I call it nabbing my nuts."

"That has a certain vivid alliteration to it," Bea said.

The construction foreman's voice dropped to a whisper as he looked past them toward the water. "I'll tell you a couple things about my house. My wife and I built it with our own hands. It took us nearly three years working nights, weekends, and vacations. The kids were small then and I wasn't even a journeyman carpenter, so money was short. I dug the foundation by hand. I mean with a pick and shovel. Our sweat built that place for twenty thousand and now it's worth a quarter of a million. I got two kids, one will come to work with me next year and learn the business that way. The other one is real bright, college material, and is going to be a civil engineer or maybe even an architect. A second mortgage on that house is going to pay for that kid's college, no matter where she wants to go. Dalton isn't taking that away from me with his asshole games and toilet barge boat, and that's a promise."

"Doesn't Pan have any influence with him?"

"She's a fucking space cadet."

"She keeps insisting that someone is threatening Dalton," Bea said. "And today someone shot at the boat."

"I'm not surprised," Sam snorted. "The guy's fucking me, his wife in more ways than one, Kat Loops, the public at large, and anyone else stupid enough to get near the loony bastard."

"You sound pissed," Lyon said.

"Mister, I'm not just pissed. I got complete kidney malfunction."

"Hey, you guys!" Pan Turman ran up the walk toward them.

"Oh, Christ," Sam said. "It's time to play Dalton says."

"Dalton says we're all to go to the ballroom," Pan said breathlessly as she tried to regain her wind. "He has something to show us."

"Does Dalton say who's to supervise this fucking job while we play his damn games?" Sam said.

Pan hooked the foreman's arm in hers as she led him up the path toward the large building. "Oh, Sam, you're such a grizzly bear."

The southerly wall of the ballroom was mostly glass, with sliding panels that opened out onto a wide veranda that overlooked Long Island Sound. The ceiling was a maze of molded figure reliefs, many parts of which had broken off and fallen to the cluttered floor. The walls were water stained, and plaster, leaves, and old newspapers littered the floor.

The restoration was well under way. Scaffolding reached high up the walls and contained several painters who were carefully chipping and sanding the orante molding. Lyon noticed that several of the younger workers had Walkman radios either hooked to their belts or sitting nearby. Luckily they used earphones so that the sound of heavy-metal rock was mercifully absent.

"This is my favorite room in the whole resort," Pan said. "Later I'll show you the decorator's drawings of what it will look like when it's finished."

Sam Idelweise began to impatiently riffle through a sheaf of blueprints. "Where's laughing boy?" he muttered.

"I'll go get him," Pan said and hurried out.

"Oh, my God!" It was a strangulated gasp from one of the men working near the ceiling. The young painter scrambled down the ladder. He wore a Grateful Dead T-shirt, paint-splattered, cutoff jeans, and carried a blaster with an earplug. He reached the bottom of the ladder and faced them with a look of horror on his face. "It's coming! Jesus, they're finally on their way."

Sam scowled at the young worker. "No breaks for the second coming, Harold. You wait for lunch like everyone else."

Harold ripped the earplug from his head and threw it at Idelweise. His mouth opened and closed several times before words were articulated. "I don't care what you say. It doesn't matter anymore. Don't you understand? The missiles are on their way!"

"What in the hell are you talking about?" Idelweise shot back.

"It's all on the radio. Listen!" Harold turned up the set's volume.

All work stopped as a sonorous announcer's voice filled the ballroom. "The Pentagon has verified that countless missiles have been launched from areas throughout the

Soviet Union. Early-warning satellites indicated that this occurred sixteen minutes ago." The announcer's hysteria was becoming obvious and beginning to affect everyone in the ballroom.

"Civil Defense officials recommend that everyone stay away from windows and . . . It doesn't matter what you do, it's all over. This is the end."

The broadcast abruptly terminated.

Sam Idelweise strode purposefully across the room. "No way! No way, José, do I believe this shit." His booted foot lashed out and smashed into the radio.

The appliance's owner looked dispassionately down at the ruined set and shook his head. "It doesn't matter. Nothing matters."

Sam shook the young painter by the shoulders. "Snap out of it, kid. That bastard Dalton is up to another of his . . ."

Everyone in the room froze in a silent tableau as the blinding light outside the window cascaded through the room in one gigantic flash.

"Mother of God," Sam said. "That was New York City."

"We have New York City a hundred twenty miles away to the south and Boston the same distance to the north," Lyon said. "And we're only twenty miles from New London, where the Electric Boat Company, the sub base, and the Coast Guard Academy are located."

"I don't think I need a geography lesson, Wentworth," Bea said huskily.

"We're history," Sam said.

"I love you, Lyon," Bea said as she wound her arms around him.

4 A bright light flashed again and then again.
   "Perfect. Absolutely perfect," Dalton Turman
   said from the doorway. "It has exceeded my
   fondest dreams." The flash on his Polaroid camera winked again.

Sam Idelweise blinked. "What?"

"As I would have expected," Dalton said. "The Wentworths are locked in a final embrace while Idelweise is
standing there looking dumb. Harold, I do believe you
have wet your pants." The flash blinked again. "Now,
there's an interesting reaction." He turned the camera toward a corner of the room. The girl's brimmed painter
hat had fallen to the floor and her long hair, released from

its bondage, fell down her back. She was locked in the embrace of a young male painter. His hands tore at her blouse, while her fingers under his shirt clawed at his back as she pressed against him. "Smile for the birdy, Bambi, honey," Dalton said as he snapped another picture and laughed. "Now you can go ahead and finish."

Sam reached into a large toolbox to pick up a hammer. "I'm going to kill the son of a bitch!" He started toward Dalton, who turned and ran from the room.

"Stop them, Lyon!" Bea said in alarm.

When Lyon reached the outside of the building, Dalton was halfway down the path leading to the water. Sam was not far behind and seemed to be gaining. The construction foreman bellowed and waved the hammer over his head.

Dalton reached the water steps ahead of Sam, and without breaking stride, ran into the bay and dove. He swam twenty strong strokes before turning to tred water.

Sam stood waist-deep in the water with the hammer still raised. Lyon reached for the weapon. "Easy, Sam." Idelweise snatched the hammer away with a glare.

"I knew the bear couldn't swim," Dalton called. "Uh-oh." He quickly ducked underwater as the hammer arced through the air and landed where his head had been.

"I swear to God, I'm going to get that sucker," Sam said before he stomped from the water and back toward the main building.

Dalton surfaced and waved at Lyon. "Get my camera, will you? And have Bobby take the boat out a hundred yards with everyone aboard except Sam. I'll meet you guys out there."

"That man should be quarantined on an uninhabited island," Bea said as she climbed aboard the houseboat.

"Do you know where Bobby is?" Lyon asked as he followed his wife aboard.

"They told me he was on board. Let's look in his stateroom."

They walked through the main saloon and back toward the rooms. The last door was slightly ajar. There was a couple on the bunk.

Katrina Loops did not have on her string bikini, in fact neither she nor Bobby Douglas wore anything. Lyon and Bea quickly turned and hurried back down the hall but not before they were viewed with alarm by the embracing couple.

"Wait!" Katrina rushed down the companionway after them, wrapping a large terry-cloth towel around her large frame as she ran. She clutched at Bea's arm. "Please don't say anything to anyone. Please."

"We didn't intend to," Bea answered.

She turned to Lyon. "He'd kill me if he thought I was doing it with anyone else." The woman had momentarily lost any vestiges of sophistication, and had reverted to a teenager's fear of authority.

"Not a word," Lyon promised.

She looked at each of them a moment, clutched the towel tightly around her neck, and then hurried back down the hall.

"I have questions," Bea said when they were seated on deck under the awning. "Would Sam have bludgeoned Dalton to death if he had caught him during that wild chase?"

"The way I read Sam, he would have beaten the hell out of Dalton, but not killed him."

"Maybe true over the practical joke," Bea said. "But in other areas I'm not so sure."

"My question," said Lyon, "is, if Katrina is so concerned about Dalton finding out she's having an affair with Bobby, why in the hell do they do it in the middle of the day on Dalton's boat with the door open?"

"I think she wanted Pan to walk in on them," Bea said.

"Ah, that was the game plan."

"An ancient method of hiding the real reason for suspicion," Bea said.

"What have you heard about Douglas? I don't believe Dalton's story about running drugs."

"Pandora tells me that he's a ranked tennis player and will be the pro here at the resort when it opens. He's crewing this barge only until his leg tendon mends. Let's see if we can find a drink. I need something to help me recover from World War Three."

Dalton changed clothes, but not before closing the drapes in the main saloon and insisting that they all sit Indian fashion on the floor. No one commented on the unorthodox seating, but they all knew that it gave them protection from possible gunfire.

"Isn't anyone going to talk to me?" Dalton asked.

"No one wants to talk to you and Sam wants to kill you," Pan said. "Bambi was so embarrassed that she ran off the job crying hysterically that the only reason she tried to do it was because she didn't want to die a virgin."

"What!" Dalton yelled. "Bambi was a virgin? Why wasn't I told? I would have demanded the right of *droit du seigneur.* Where's my camera?"

"I threw it in the water! You jerk!"

Dalton smiled bitterly. "That wasn't a very nice thing for Miss Conviviality to do."

"Oh, stop it! I was never Miss Conviviality and you know it. The only votes I ever got were from my high-school football team when they selected me as Miss Community Chest, and I'll leave that one to your imagination."

"That was a convincing trick you played on us," Lyon interjected to relieve tension. "How did you do it?"

Dalton preened. "One out-of-work actor, a tape recorder, and some radio equipment from Radio Shack. That was the easy part. It took me three nights' work to get the magnesium placed properly outside the ballroom. Synchronizing its explosion with a trigger device was a little complicated, but worth it. If you could only have seen your faces . . . You really shouldn't have destroyed my camera, Pan. That's a no-no."

"Oh, shut up!"

"At least my friends appreciate me," Dalton said as he smiled at Bea.

Pan went rigid. Her fists clenched as she stood angrily before her husband. "Your friends! You don't have any friends. The Wentworths are practically the only people left on this planet who will give you the time of day. And they only see you once a year and during that time you succeed in doing perfectly dreadful things to them."

"It will only cost a couple of hundred dollars to repair the holes in the kitchen wall that Rocco made," Bea said.

"And even Lyon would probably hit you if he wasn't so grateful over that business during the war," Pan continued.

"What war was that?" Katrina asked.

"*The War* is always the one the men present fought in," Bea said.

"That time-sharing business doesn't sound so bad," Lyon said in a valiant attempt to change the direction of the conversation. "Katrina gave us the full sales pitch, and the ability to swap units for a week anywhere in the world does sound intriguing."

Dalton harumphed. "Sure, if you care for Timbuktu in the dead of winter, or if high summer in Death Valley grabs you."

"No one can be that cynical," Katrina said with a laugh.

"It has nothing to do with cynicism," the developer said. "I call it reality orientation, survival of the fittest, or as the bumper sticker on my Mercedes says, 'He who has the most toys at the end wins.'"

As Bobby Douglas gently docked the *Mississippi* on the river across from Nutmeg Hill, they saw a heavyset man in a business suit standing impatiently on the lip of the ancient pier. He had taken off his suit jacket and had it hooked over his shoulder with his finger as a foot tapped the planking. His whole body seemed to will a faster progress of the houseboat's mooring.

"Why do I have this strong feeling that Mr. Dice wishes to have words with me?" Dalton asked.

"Because I can tell by the way he's acting that you've screwed him again, darling," Pan answered sweetly.

"Yonder impatient man is Randy Dice, my partner and chief financial officer," Dalton said to Lyon. "He has this insane compulsion to make our balance sheets actually balance."

"I can't wait to depart from this craft of joy," Bea whispered in Lyon's ear.

Dice dropped his jacket and jumped to the deck of the houseboat before the lines had been secured. Bobby stood at the bow holding a coiled rope. He shrugged and leaped the short distance to the pier and began to complete the docking alone. Dice hurried toward Dalton.

"You lied to me again!" His voice cracked with intensity.

"Probably," Dalton said with his usual skewered smile. "If it's about being the father of your children, I have already talked to your wife about that."

"I'm in no mood for your frivolous jokes. I went to the bank today."

"It seems to me that you often go to the bank. In fact, Randy, you are always going to the bank."

"They asked me about the sale of your West Hartford house. A clerk picked up the deed transfer during a routine check of the week's recordings. That house was one of the items we pledged as loan collateral. I gave my word. I signed disclosure statements and notes to that effect. My word and reputation are on the line, and you sold it out from under us and never deposited the money in our corporate accounts."

"It slipped my mind."

"This is the end, Dalton. I warned you. I am finished. I resign from the corporation effective immediately."

"Let us reason together, my boy," Dalton said as he took the irate businessman's arm and led him across the deck away from the others. Dice seemed to shrink as he listened to Dalton, and after a short conversation he stepped back on the pier and began to walk slowly up the hill to his parked car. His suit jacket lay on the planking where he had discarded it.

"Is he leaving the company?" Pan asked as Dalton rejoined them.

"I think not. I believe I have persuaded Mr. Dice that it is in his best interests to remain a member of our cozy organization."

"Okay people," Pan said exuberantly, "let's go ashore."

"And where in the hell do you think you're going? We live on this thing now," Dalton said.

"Not me, sweety," Pan said. "Miss Conviviality will not sleep here tonight, and maybe not even tomorrow night."

They were a subdued trio as they drove back down the river to the bridge. Lyon was at the wheel with Bea at his side, while a very quiet Pan sat in the rear seat. Bea had tried to make conversation, but the lack of response had quickly stifled the attempt. Bobby and Katrina had driven off in the resort's station wagon claiming a host of errands. They had left Dalton standing on the upper deck with a drink in his hand, staring sullenly down at them.

"You're welcome to stay the night at Nutmeg Hill," Bea said in her second attempt at dialogue.

"I don't want to be a bother," Pan replied. "I have a

cottage at the resort where I can stay. I think I'd rather be alone tonight to do some serious thinking."

"I understand," Bea answered. "Borrow our car."

"Wake up, Wentworth!"

He winked open one eye to see Bea bent over him bathed in bright moonlight. She poked him in the ribs. "What is?" he managed to mumble.

"Someone is downstairs pounding on the front door."

"Equal rights say you go." He pulled the pillow over his head.

"I would, except that it's probably your large policeman friend here to discuss some interesting case."

"Okay." He stumbled from bed and toward the door. "What time is it?"

"It's three A.M., and in case it isn't Rocco down there, you had better put something on."

"Oh, ya." He realized he was nude and reached into the closet to snick a robe from its hook. He slipped it on and belted it. "You know, I think Katrina looked better in the string bikini than she did *au naturel.*"

"At this stage of life you should know that all of us look slightly ludicrous in that position. Go answer the door."

Pandora Turman was leaning against the house near the front door as she mechanically raised and lowered the large brass doorknocker.

"You didn't have to return our car this early," Lyon said before he realized the inanity of the remark.

"He's gone. I went back to where the boat was docked and Dalton is gone."

"He probably went into town."

"You don't understand, Lyon. The *Mississippi* is gone. The whole houseboat has disappeared."

5 They stood in moonlight on the patio and took
turns looking through the telescope. They swept
the river in both directions until their vision
was obscured by its change in course.

"I can't see it," Bea said, "and it would be hard to miss
something that large."

Pan paced nervously behind them. "I went to our cottage back at the resort, but I couldn't get to sleep worry-
ing about how much financial pressure Dalton's been
under lately. I decided to go back to him and drove back
down here. When I couldn't find the boat, I just thought
he'd moved it for some reason. I drove up the river to
Hartford, and back all the way to the Sound. I can't find it.
He's gone."

"Let me check it out with Rocco," Lyon said. "He's our local police chief." He went into the kitchen and dialed the wall phone. The call was answered on the first ring. "I have a problem," he said without preamble.

"When you call at three in the morning and I'm still awake, we both have problems."

"Dalton Turman is missing."

"Is that a promise?"

"I'm serious. The guy and his boat are gone. His wife is here and she's worried sick. She doesn't deserve that, Rocco."

"Her marriage proves that she's paying for terrible sins from past lives. She must have been Typhoid Mary."

"I'm calling you as a friend who happens to be a police officer."

"Did it ever occur to you why I'm awake? I will tell you why. I am trying to create a DD twenty-three—forty-one."

"What's that?"

"An official form called, 'Unauthorized Discharge of a Firearm.' Copies go to the Mayor, the State Police, and the state. You're the writer, tell me how to explain why I was at a party, drinking pepper vodka, and then chose to empty a Magnum at a dish cabinet filled with large snakes. You don't happen to have any snake remains around, do you?"

"We sent them to the dump, but we still have the bullet holes in the wall."

"That won't help. All right, how long has Dalton been gone?"

"A couple of hours."

"I can't start an official investigation for at least twenty-four hours, and you know his tricks never last that long."

"He's had threats, and today someone took a shot at us."

"I haven't seen any official reports of a shot, and as far

as threats are concerned, not only is Dalton Prankenstein, he is also a builder. In his case, threats should be expected. If you think the bad guys are after him, you're really a glutton for punishment."

"The houseboat seems to be gone."

"It's either on the river or on the Sound. If we're really lucky, he's in Spain by now."

"I repeat," Lyon said, "someone shot at us on the boat today with a high-powered rifle."

"You *thought* someone fired at you. That's easy enough to stage. You know, this guy is going to keep chewing you up until you stop playing his games." Rocco paused, waiting for Lyon's agreement. When it wasn't forthcoming, he continued. "Okay, if you're going to spend the rest of the night looking for the *Mississippi,* you might try the bridges. That barge is as big as a damn destroyer and can't go upstream or out into the Sound without making it past a bridge. Do you know the ones I mean?"

"Yes, there's one upstream from us at Haddam's Neck, and another at the mouth of the river."

"Right, and either one would have to be opened for the *Mississippi.* They're manned twenty-four hours a day, and the operator keeps a log on each opening. Go talk to bridges while I try and invent a good story about snakes."

Lyon had prepared a hot Thermos before they left the house, and they drank coffee as they drove toward the Haddam's Neck bridge. Pandora cupped a plastic mug with both hands and spoke in a quiet voice that was far removed from her earlier staccato speech.

"Something terrible has happened to him or he has decided to leave me."

"Or he's going to let us spend all day looking before he appears with a drink in his hand and that damn laugh of his."

"Either that rotten man who calls at night has gotten him or he's run off with his new girlfriend." She glanced at Lyon with a feline ferocity. "A woman can always tell when her man is doing it with someone else. If I ever catch them together, I'll kill him and tear her face off."

"There are other alternatives, Pan," Lyon said. "You had a minor argument and in a fit of pique he hid the boat in a cove. If he didn't pass through either of the bridges, we'll know he slipped into a dock area near here."

"Will these help?" She handed him a packet of photographs. "Dalton took these to send to some boat magazine."

Lyon glanced down at the spread of color photographs taken of the houseboat from a score of different distances, heights, and angles. "They'll be a big help." He reached over to squeeze her fingers, but her hands were tightly clutching the dashboard.

"He just better be busted up by baseball bats," she said. "If I find him in the saddle with some bimbo, he's dead meat."

The Haddam's Neck bridge was of ancient steel-girder construction that seemed to form a confusing maze of beams above the roadbed. At the direction of the operator, perched in a control shack high in the superstructure, the entire center section could be swiveled in order to allow large boats to pass through.

They parked the car near the entrance to the bridge and walked out over the water. The river below shimmered in the thinning darkness as clouds of predawn haze began to rise from its surface. In both directions, the only visible craft was a single fishing boat moving slowly downstream with upright naked rods swaying gently in metal brackets near the stern. They reached the center of the bridge where a metal ladder led up to the small booth nestled high among the girders.

Pan craned her neck to look up the vertical ladder. "I can't go up there," she said. "Would you mind going alone?"

Lyon did mind, but without answering, he gripped the cool metal rungs of the ladder and began to climb. In recent years his fear of heights had increased geometrically with his age. For reasons he could not understand, a flight in his hot-air balloon did not bother him, but climbing a ladder slick with river mist scared the hell out of him. He did not look down.

His head topped the window glass of the control room and he looked inside to see the operator bent over a desk. A discreet knock would require releasing one frantic grip from the ladder. He considered the problem a moment, and then banged his forehead against the glass.

The bridge operator looked up at Lyon with a startled glance and then vehemently shook his head. "You can't come in! Authorized personnel only, so beat it before I call the cops . . . unless you got a cigarette?"

"Always carry a couple extra packs," Lyon lied. The door was thrust back against the wall and two hands helped Lyon into the small room. "Have you opened the bridge tonight?"

"I open the bridge, I close the bridge, and in between I read a lot of books and try not to think about cigarettes. Where are they, for God's sake?!"

"I'm looking for a large houseboat called the *Mississippi*," Lyon said.

"Don't usually have to move the bridge for houseboats, they're too low in the water. Hope you got some real cigarettes, no filters, no low nicotine. I need a real lung grabber."

Lyon began to pat his pockets in a fruitless search for the photographs and nonexistent cigarettes. "This boat has a high superstructure and mast. I'll show you a picture when I find them."

The operator pointed to the open door. "I don't look at nothing without a burning coffin nail in my hand. Get your pictures and there's a cigarette machine in the restaurant vestibule at the far end of the bridge."

Lyon closed his eyes as he stepped outside.

The second operator was located on the railroad bridge near the mouth of the Connecticut River. Somehow, Lyon's appearance at the control-room window seemed quite natural to him, and he waved a friendly greeting while simultaneously shoving his pint of rye into a desk drawer.

He bent over the desk where Lyon spread the *Mississippi* photographs and squinted at them. Still not satisfied with his focus, he covered one eye with the flat of his hand. "Nope. I'd remember that baby. Only things I opened for tonight were a coastal tanker and a large motor sailboat."

Lyon reluctantly gathered the photographs. "Thanks anyway."

"Wait a minute!" The operator flipped back a page in the bridge log. "Here are two entries for a large houseboat."

"Where?" Lyon eagerly bent over the book.

"She went out yesterday morning and came back later in the day."

"We know about that trip," Lyon said, for it was obviously their round-trip excursion to the resort the day before. "Thanks anyway. I'd be appreciative if you told me of another way to get down from here."

"Sure." Lyon smiled. He wasn't ready for another bout with the ladder. "You can jump," the operator said with a laugh.

"We've bracketed the *Mississippi*," Lyon told Pan when he was back in the car. "We know she didn't go up- or downstream past the bridges."

She looked doubtful. "Dalton once told me that he could buy anyone if the price was right. How much do bridge operators go for?"

"I've considered that," Lyon said. "I don't think either of the operators were lying to me, but I have a way to double-check. The U.S. Army Corps of Engineers has a channel dredger near Haddam that operates twenty-four hours a day. I'll also check with the Coast Guard at Lynde Point on the Sound. It will only take a couple of phone calls to verify what we've learned. Even Dalton couldn't have reached all of them."

"I suppose you're right," she said dubiously.

"The boat has to be moored somewhere between the two bridges, in a cove, at a marina, or in open water. It's one of those choices."

"I hear what you're saying, but I have a very bad feeling about this."

Bea's legs flicked through the opening of her bathrobe as she strode angrily across the kitchen and thunked down two coffee mugs on the breakfast table. "And where is Miss Conviviality now?"

"In our guest room. She's pretty well zonked out, but she made me promise to wake her as soon as the plane arrives."

Bea's sugar spoon missed her mug by several inches. Powdery grains scattered across the table. "The *what?*"

"I've rented a float plane for the morning. I thought that would be the best way to explore the coves and marinas along this stretch of river."

"And your seaplane will taxi to a landing at the foot of our promontory where you and Miss 'C' will be waiting hand in hand." She sipped coffee. "Do you ever intend to finish your book?"

"It hasn't been going too well lately," Lyon said and was surprised to see his two Wobblies standing in the doorway and beckoning frantically for him to return to the study.

"You know he's pulling another prank and you're going to feel like a horse's ass falling for three in a row. Does Pan realize how much this plane ride is going to cost her?"

"A hundred an hour plus miscellaneous fees."

"For some people it's easy come, easy go."

"Well, actually she's a little short at the moment," Lyon said. "I know that Dalton will repay me when it's over."

Bea looked stricken. "We're paying for chartered airplanes?"

"Dalton's good for it."

"Sure, like he was good about paying for the bullet holes in our kitchen wall."

"I've been thinking about those holes," Lyon said. "Since Rocco fired a tight shot pattern in a downward trajectory, we could cut a larger hole around the little holes and make a door for a cat."

"I might remind you that we don't have a cat."

"They're easy to come by."

"And that the last cat we had ate twelve hundred birds." A seaplane banked over the house and turned downwind for a river landing. "Your transportation is here, Wentworth," Bea said. "Have a nice day in Oz."

Gary Dorset inched the float plane to the base of the promontory below Nutmeg Hill and tossed a line over a dead branch that protruded from the water. He climbed down to the right pontoon wearing a scuffed, leather flying jacket with a large American flag sewn on the back. He waved at Lyon and Pan as they picked their way down the winding path.

"Fine morning for a sortie, hey, Terry?" the pilot called.

"Righto," Lyon yelled back.

"I'm not so sure I want to fly with him," Pan whispered. "I think he's flaky."

"He's just a little eccentric," Lyon whispered back. "In the morning he likes to play Flying Tiger. In the afternoon he puts on a business suit and flies canceled checks to the Federal Reserve Bank in Boston."

Dorset leaned forward to take Pandora's hand and help her board the plane. "Don't get your feet wet, Dragon Lady." He turned to help Lyon. "If I know you, this must have something to do with murder. Who's been knocked off?"

"Would you believe a missing houseboat? We think it's lost somewhere between the two bridges. Pan, show him the photographs of the boat."

Dorset climbed into the cockpit and let the plane drift into the current as he examined the pictures. "A cake walk," he said. "We shall find the missing sampan and call the mission a success." He handed back the pictures and flipped switches. "It's not as if we have to fly the Yangtze with Zeroes diving out of the sun."

He started the engine and they turned into the current to begin the takeoff run. "I'll take the downstream railway bridge as a starting point," Dorset continued. "You watch the right side, the lady the left, and I'll fly midstream. Clear!"

Lyon almost yelled, "Tallyho," but suppressed the impulse.

Flying at near stall speed, they made round trips from one bridge to another and back again without seeing anything that faintly resembled the *Mississippi*. On the third leg, Dorset flew over every estuary and inlet large enough to admit the large houseboat. The results were negative.

One marina, located near the town of Wessex, looked promising. It had metal tracks leading up from the water into a large shed that was large enough to enclose the *Mississippi.*

Dorset flew across the river opposite the large marina shed, banked sharply, and approached the building at a height that was only a few feet above the water. When they were less than a hundred yards from the facility, Lyon saw through its open doors that it contained a twelve-meter sailboat with an unstepped mast. The craft's sleek configurations were far different than the *Mississippi's* square lines.

The seaplane seemed destined to fly directly into the building, until at the last possible moment, Dorset jerked back on the stick and threw the plane into a shuddering climb that cleared the building by inches.

"She isn't on the river," the pilot yelled over the roar of the engine as the plane fought for altitude. "The house-boat sure isn't here unless . . ."

"Unless what?" Pan asked.

"Unless it's under the water," Dorset replied as he threw the plane into a steep banking turn.

The two men glared at each other across the small of-fice as if they represented the Cattlemen's Association and the Sheepherders' Benevolent Society. Captain Norbert, commander of the local State Police barracks, had a natu-ral antipathy toward local law-enforcement officers. In the case of Rocco Herbert, the feeling was exacerbated by the fact that the two men were brothers-in-law.

Lyon slouched in a chair by Rocco's desk with tented fingers as he waited for the mutual antagonism to subside.

"Run that DD twenty-three—forty-one by me again, Herbert," Norbert said. "Tell me once more why you dis-charged a three-fifty-seven Magnum in a civilian dwell-ing."

"Tell him about the snakes, Lyon," Rocco said.

"What snakes?" Lyon answered ingenuously.

"I've told you before, Rocco," Norbert said. "You've got to lay off the damn vodka! This is the last time I'll cover for you. Now, what in the hell have you done about the missing-person report?"

Rocco shrugged. "Not much."

"So I gather. I didn't see any search efforts when I came in here. I don't see any maps on walls. I don't see any banks of telephones. In fact, I don't see anything going on around here! You locals are all right as school-crossing guards, but when something important comes along you need the professionals."

"Do you know who's missing, Norbie?" Rocco asked.

"I sure in hell do! He's one of the most prominent developers in the state. As a matter of fact, the wife and I are thinking seriously of buying one of his time-sharing units." He leaned forward with a prurient glint. "The broad who gave us the sales pitch must have been seven feet tall and built like a brick slammer."

"Let me get out the crayons," Rocco said. "Do you remember a call five years ago when we went out to the Willow house on the turnpike to investigate a mass murder?"

"Jesus, do I! We found body parts all over the goddamn place. And I've never seen so much gore. Corporal Hennegan, who was tough enough to face down Mad Dog Majeski, was so traumatized that we had to hospitalize him."

"And what was the outcome of that carnage?"

"The Medical Examiner told us later that the body parts were from sides of beef, and the other junk was sheep entrails. A lot of good that did for the guys who had already barfed. I know you got the bastard who set us up, and I like to think that the other cons in max security did a number on him."

"You tell him," Rocco said. "I've been avoiding it for years."

"It was plea-bargained down to mischievous mischief and he got off with accelerated rehabilitation," Lyon said.

"No hard time?"

"Not day one," Rocco said. "And that's Dalton Turman, the prominent builder and our missing person. That's the guy you want command centers and overtime for."

Norbert stood, enraged. "Why wasn't I told?"

"He could be dead," Lyon said.

"So? You've already got his coffin," Rocco replied.

"I saw a guy on TV make a seven-forty-seven airplane disappear," Norbert said.

"Houdini made an elephant disappear off a New York City stage," Rocco added.

"Come on," Lyon said. "I'm worried about him. I think he's really gone." Lyon saw the complete lack of compassion on the two police officers' faces.

Rocco picked up a file folder. "The request will have to be instituted by family members with complete documentation."

"The paperwork will be horrendous," Norbert said with an unpleasant smile. "If the case ever gets to my office, I'll put Corporal Murphy right on it."

"I didn't realize he was back from the drunk farm," Rocco said.

"Occasionally," Norbert answered. He stood and flicked dust from his spit-shined shoes. "I should have known. Every time I get involved with Wentworth it means trouble."

"Get yourself ready for the Governor's call," Lyon said to the State Police captain.

"What are you talking about?" Norbert snapped.

"My wife is presently involved in very delicate negotiations with the Governor. Suffice it to say that he would like her cooperation in certain matters. I do believe that you may expect a personal phone call from the Governor, the commissioner, and your immediate supervisor, the major." Lyon sat back in the chair and retented his fingers knowing that Bea would ask such a favor from the Governor as readily as she'd join the Nazi party.

"Not the major," Rocco said. "Even you aren't that much of a bastard."

"Can he do it?" Norbert asked Rocco.

"I was at their house when the Governor called," Rocco said. "He was begging Bea, Norbie. Begging. Lyon's got us by the short hairs, and if you're lucky, you won't get a reprimand, and if I'm lucky, maybe he'll tell you about the snakes."

Lyon intently leaned forward. "Now, here's what I've done so far." He outlined his conversations with the bridge operators, the follow-up phone calls to the Army Corps of Engineers and the Coast Guard station at Lynde Point. He described the airplane flight and the subsequent automobile trips he and Pan had made.

Rocco spoke first. "I'll assign cars to search the riverbank in Murphysville."

"State cruisers will handle the rest," Norbert said. "You know, Wentworth, this joker has probably jacked the thing out of the water and hidden it."

"There's only a dozen or so places in this area where something that large could be hauled ashore," Rocco said.

"We'll never find it if someone's sunk it," Lyon mumbled.

"I'll call Coast Guard Operations in New London," Norbert said. "They have a cutter equipped with sounding gear and scuba divers trained for just such a search."

"I'll coordinate that with Army charts," Rocco added. "The river is considered navigable in this area, so the Corps of Engineers has to keep the channel open. Their charts will pinpoint every spot deep enough to scuttle the damn thing. We're going to find the bastard for you, Lyon, but when we do, it's boom-lowering time."

"He'll never drive on a Connecticut highway, that's for sure," Norbert said with satisfaction.

"I'm going up," Lyon said.

Bea snapped a weed from the garden and stared at the offending vegetation with distaste. "If anyone else made that statement, I'd think mood-altering substances. With you, I think balloons."

"I need a good panoramic view of the river to give me a clue as to how that boat disappeared."

"I suppose it would be useless to suggest that we let the police and Coast Guard handle it?"

"So far they've come up with zilch."

She spotted another weed two rows away and lunged for it. "Might I remind you of your last balloon excursion."

"I remember that it was a slightly overcast day with a few cumulus and a five-mile-an-hour wind from the north."

"I am referring to the incident between your balloon and Air Force One."

"I still say I had the right of way. It's sail over steam, you know."

"The Secret Service didn't quite see it that way."

"Those guys have no sense of humor."

The *Wobbly II* was a large hot-air balloon that stretched over eighty feet from the apex of the bag's envelope to the passenger gondola. Bea's heels were dug into the dirt and her body nearly horizontal to the ground as she strained to hold the anchor rope that kept the inflated balloon earthbound. Lyon climbed into the wicker basket and reached overhead to pull the propane release lever to give the burner a five-second burst of flame. He signaled his wife and she let go of the anchor rope.

The balloon immediately bounced vertically into the air as Lyon coiled the anchor rope neatly in the boot of the gondola. Buoyed by a full complement of hot air, the balloon rose noiselessly without the necessity of further propane burns.

He found the ascent exhilarating as he had countless times before. At twenty-one-hundred feet it began to slow and bob, and he gave a short tug on the burner lever to maintain that altitude. The wind was from the east, and the balloon began to drift slowly along the meandering course of the Connecticut River.

He leaned his elbows on the basket rail while the binoculars hanging from his neck swayed gently in the craft's slight movement. The river, two thousand feet below, curved gently as it wound its way from the Atlantic Ocean to the Canadian border. The riverbanks between the two bridges were largely bracketed by wooded hills that rose abruptly from the shore. There were only a few open fields or launching ramps where the large *Mississippi* could have been winched ashore.

It had been two days since the meeting in Rocco's office. During that time, both the Murphysville Police and state cruisers had been busy. Police cars had driven down every road in the area that led to the river or that ran parallel to the water. Using Corps of Engineers charts, the Coast Guard had made soundings, and on several occasions dropped scuba divers into the water to investigate promising leads.

The Coast Guard was now convinced that the houseboat had not been scuttled in this section of the river, and they had called off their search. State and local police were equally certain that the *Mississippi* had not been lifted ashore, hidden, or trucked from the area.

Lyon was puzzled at the impossible situation. Objects as large and cumbersome as the *Mississippi* did not disappear. It was as if the boat had been dematerialized or snatched from the water's surface by some unknown power.

Was it possible that it had been hoisted aloft? He had read of large work helicopters that were capable of lifting huge loads on steel cables. Could Dalton have arranged . . .

Basic mathematics precluded the possibility. To fly an object as large as the *Mississippi* would require a machine of impossible size.

The bridge operators, their logs, and other sources all agreed that the only two large vessels seen on the river the night of the disappearance were a sailing ship and a coastal tanker. Neither craft was large enough to have winched all or part of the *Mississippi* aboard.

If the houseboat hadn't been sunk, hidden along the waterfront, or trucked from the area, what had happened to it? Arthur Conan Doyle wrote, in "A Study in Scarlet," that, "When you have eliminated the impossible, whatever remains, however improbable, must be the truth."

There was one improbable possibility to be explored.

Lyon excitedly snatched the walkie-talkie clipped to the gondola's side and switched it on. "Hello, chase car. *Wobbly* is ready to descend."

The other radio crackled a moment before Bea's voice transmitted clearly. "Glad to hear it, *Wobbly*. The State Senate would very much like to go into session this afternoon."

"I see a large open field directly beneath me on your side of the river," Lyon said. "I will pull my ripping panel for a rapid descent. Over."

"Don't, *Wobbly!*" Bea shouted. "Don't pull the panel . . . Uh-oh, you've already done it. You are about to drop in on Victorian Acres, Wentworth. Lots of luck. Out."

Lyon glanced at the corner of the basket to make sure that the bottle of champagne was intact. Due to the haphazard nature of balloon landings, it was age-old custom for descending balloonists to offer wine to those in their landing areas. Most people were pleased at the diversion.

When the balloon broke one hundred feet and continued a rapid descent, Lyon saw men and women playing volleyball in the field below. He instantly realized why Bea was concerned, and he gripped the sides of the basket tightly. He hoped the champagne would assuage their feelings.

The balloon basket made a bumpy landing and Lyon levered a small propane burn to keep the gondola upright. He popped the champagne cork and leaned over the basket with wine foaming over his fingers. "We balloonists have an ancient landing rule," he said as he held up the bottle.

"We have rules too, creep," the largest man in the group of naked people said.

"Start shucking clothes, corn pone," his feminine companion added.

The Governor's voice was unctuous. "It's only because of past favors that they came to me with the information first."

"What was said?" Bea asked. His gratuitous offer of confidential information meant that she was probably on the brink of utter disaster.

"Unimpeachable sources inform me that your husband was seen cavorting in the nude with that bunch at Victorian Acres."

Bea hadn't seen Lyon cavort since the twist went out of fashion, but then she had refused to drive the chase car inside the confines of the nudist camp. "Cavorting, Governor?"

"You know there's been talk of sexual orgies out there."

"There's a rather complicated explanation for what happened," Bea said.

"I'm sure there is, Senator. Perhaps we can discuss it over lunch tomorrow?"

"Yes, we'll do that." She had already replaced the phone in its cradle when she realized that she had neglected the obvious question. Who had observed Lyon's antics within the fenced, guarded, and heavily wooded colony? She sometimes felt that she wasn't nearly tough enough for cut-throat politics. "Lyon, have you been cavorting again?" she called out. "One of the Governor's spies saw you at Victorian Acres in an orgy."

He wandered into the room. "It was volleyball. Volleyball is evidently *de rigeur,* the same as taking off your clothes. Someone's in the drive, it must be Gary Dorset."

"Please, no more expensive plane rides."

"I'm not going up," he said as he went to the front door. He saw that Dorset was driving a Jeep with a large FOLLOW ME sign on its rear. That was a good omen. When the pilot got out of the Jeep, he carried a leather briefcase and wore his going-to-the-Federal-Reserve banker's suit. That was a bad omen.

Pan, Lyon, and Bea sat quietly in the study while Dorset opened the briefcase that straddled his knees. He carefully pulled out an invoice. "As I understand it, you want an aerial map of the area you outlined for me? Good aerial photography requires a stable platform, so I'll have to take the two-engine Cesna. We'll also need an experienced copilot to operate and load the cameras. There are extra costs for the camera rentals, film, developing, and so forth."

"Do you have any numbers?" Lyon asked.

"It's all included in the estimate," Dorset said as he handed the bill to Lyon.

"Do it," Lyon said. "I need that aerial map as soon as possible."

Dorset strode to the door. "I fly at dawn!"

Bea looked at the pilot's estimate. "Do we have to do this?" Lyon nodded. "We'll have to sell my soul to pay for it. I wonder what state senator souls go for these days."

"Don't be Faustian, dear," Lyon said.

"Faust? You're talking Faust and the devil! I'm talking really serious trouble—the Governor." She started up the stairs. "I have to get ready for work. You two, spend no more money!"

Lyon smiled after her as she left and then turned to Pan. "Did you find Dalton's address book?"

She held up a dog-eared red volume. "I found this in his desk at the resort office. There may be another one on the houseboat. I've gone through it and put a mark next to the people I know, but there's a whole bunch of other names that don't mean anything to me. None of them say gravel-voice man who calls us in the middle of the night."

Lyon pointed to the telephone. "I want you to call all the names in the book that you didn't mark off. Will you recognize the voice of the man who called at night?"

"You don't forget the sound of the man who threatens your husband."

The dusty van with the words "Pranko Construction Company" lettered on its sides came to an untidy stop at the front door. Sam Idelweise erupted into the house with a hammer raised in his right hand. "I know you're keeping the bastard here, Wentworth! I want him and I want him now!"

"I thought you threw your hammer at him the other day."

"Hammers are the only thing we have plenty of. Now produce him!"

"He's not here, but you're welcome to look."

"I will." Sam pushed past Lyon and nearly knocked Bea over as she came down the stairs.

"I don't suppose that Sam and his hammer are here to fix the holes in the kitchen?" She climbed into the Toyota and rolled down the window. "I thought not. Listen, if Dorset's aerial pictures aren't good enough, we can sell the house and get NASA to satellite-map the Eastern seaboard for us."

Lyon looked thoughtful. "If Dorset's pictures do the job we shouldn't need anything more."

"Oh, my God," Bea said as she threw the car in gear. "He really considered it." As she drove down the drive she looked in the rearview mirror and saw a man with a hammer standing on Nutmeg Hill's widow's walk. Somehow, facing the Governor didn't seem quite so appalling as it had earlier.

Lyon served a thick roast beef sandwich and an ice-cold bottle of Lowenbrau to the dejected man sitting on the patio. He joined him with a smaller sandwich for himself and an iced tea.

"He really isn't here," Sam said.

"No, and he hasn't been," Lyon replied. "Pan has been staying with us and she's now in my study making phone calls."

"Yeah, I saw her. It's been four days now, that's a little long for one of his tricks."

"He and the boat are gone. The authorities and Pan and I have searched the area and can't find a trace."

"That's not all that's missing. He's raped Pranko Construction. He's scooped up every dime there was, no matter who it belonged to."

"I thought there wasn't any money," Lyon said. "I was under the impression that the company had financial difficulties."

"He cleaned out the escrow accounts that held unit-deposit money, the payroll accounts, FICA and withholding tax accounts, you name it and he took it."

"How much did he get?"

"Dice can tell you better than I can, but it's way over a million. I had to lay off the rest of the crew yesterday, and I got this bad feeling that the paychecks are going to bounce. It's going to be sheriff time, little guys with briefcases from the state labor department time, big guys from the IRS time."

"I understand the position you're in," Lyon said.

"Do you, Wentworth? Do you really? You understand that I lose my house and everything I own, and then I go to jail? If I'm real lucky the federal people get me before the state people since federal pens are usually better. If I'm really lucky I get sent to Danbury."

"If Dalton is never found, they'll think he took everything," Lyon said. "You'll be off the hook."

"Sure, in that case I look like the biggest damn fool in the industry, and only lose my house and personal money because of the notes I signed on."

"And if Dalton is dead?" Sam munched on his sandwich, drank some beer, and looked off into space. "And if Dalton is dead?" Lyon repeated.

"Well, if they didn't find the money, the cops would think he was killed for the cash he's carrying. The insurance would cover us for everything else and get the job back on track."

"What insurance?" Lyon asked.

The construction foreman was still looking off into space. "The three of us, me, Dalton, and Dice, have partnership insurance that pays the other two if anything happens to one of us." He broke his reverie and smiled crookedly at Lyon. "Yeah, if someone would kill the son of a bitch, it would solve a lot of problems."

"You're the one who's been chasing around after him with a hammer," Lyon said.

"Hell, that's not to kill the bastard, only to knock some sense into his skull. If you're looking for bad guys, Wentworth, start thinking about Bobby Douglas. Dalton's gone, but so is that damn barge of his, and he sure didn't take it to the great practical-joke-land-in-the-sky. Who knew more about that boat than anyone else?"

"Douglas was the mate."

"He's the only one who could have made it disappear."

"Why would he do it?" Lyon asked.

"He was jumping Kat Loop's bones," Sam said.

"And Dalton . . ."

"Had a piece of that action also. In case you hadn't noticed, Kat Loops has more than enough to go around."

"Douglas has a successful tennis career," Lyon said. "He's not involved in the business end of the project."

"He'd lost it," Sam said. "Even before he hurt his leg I beat him a set. He was an over-the-hill tennis player, and that kind gets mean."

"I found it!" Pan said exuberantly from the French doors.

The segue momentarily confused Lyon, and he wondered if she was referring to Bobby's declining athletic career. "You mean the phone number?" he finally said.

She came over to the table. "After a zillion calls this guy finally answered, and as soon as he said hello I knew who it was. I'd swear it's the same voice that used to call Dalton at night."

"What in the hell is she talking about?" Sam asked.

"Did you know Dalton was into the loan sharks?" Lyon said.

Sam shrugged. "There are certain things you don't want to know."

Lyon reached for the telephone note that Pan held. "I want to call him."

Sarge's Bar and Grill was considered by all to be the raunchiest of the five establishments in Murphysville that served liquor. It was a beer-and-a-shot sort of place. In this instance, that usually meant that the owner, retired Master Sergeant Renfroe, drank a shot for every beer he served. During the day the bar was a haven for the solitary but serious drinker. Each evening Sarge turned the management over to Chester Noland, who in turn, turned the bar into the most popular gay establishment south of Hartford. It was never determined if Sarge was aware of this or simply didn't care.

Each working day at noon, Rocco Herbert ate a large hamburger in the corner booth at Sarge's. This routine had continued over the years because Sarge charged the police officer a dollar less than his other customers and prepared that particular sandwich from the finest chopped-beef tenderloin.

Lyon found Rocco at the booth and slid onto the worn wooden bench opposite the police chief. "It's been four days," he said without preamble, "and one of Dalton's irate partners was just out at the house prepared to do a little joker bashing."

"Sarge makes a great hamburger," Rocco said as he pushed his empty plate aside. "I don't know how he does it."

"Neither do I," Lyon said, knowing that any order he placed would be served from the ordinary stock of meat and therefore barely edible.

"You know, you did Norbie and me a big favor by forcing us to start the investigation of Dalton's disappearance. We both had great files to show the troops that arrived this morning."

"Who's interested in Dalton?"

"The legions have descended. You can start with the FBI, backed up by IRS auditors, surrounded by state tax and labor people with a dozen collection lawyers in tow. He's become a very popular fellow all of a sudden."

"Why the FBI?"

"They're treating it as a possible kidnapping, but that doesn't stop them from playing it both ways. In case he is still walking around, they've put his description into the computer network, are running checks on any credit-card charges he might make. I suggested they start contacting all the joke shops in the country."

"What do you mean by joke shops?"

"Most larger cities have them. The kind of places that sell exploding cigars and sneezing powder, all that good stuff that people like Dalton love."

"I think he's a little more advanced than exploding cigars."

"You never know," Rocco said. "He might need a quick joke fix one day."

"Have you ever heard of a man called Angie Carillo out of Providence?" Lyon asked.

"Boots Carillo, sure. He's Rhode Island mob. All the mob connections in this state are controlled out of Rhode Island. Carillo runs a lay-off bank and things like that."

"How about loan sharking?"

"He bankrolls, but wouldn't be personally involved unless it was big numbers," Rocco said.

"Pan found his telephone number in one of Dalton's address books and called him. She's positive that he's the one who called them at night. I thought I'd drive up there and interview him."

"You're out of your living mind," Rocco sputtered. "How in the hell do you think he got the name Boots?"

"All those guys seem to have weird nicknames like Fats, Scarface, or Needle Nose," Lyon said.

"It's street rumor that in his early days, Carillo disposed of his victims by fitting them with cement overshoes. These functioned very poorly when you tried to walk across Narragansett Bay."

"It's only a short drive."

"No way," Rocco said. "No Boots Carillo and no trips to Rhode Island. Got it?"

"No trip to Providence, got it," Lyon repeated.

It took Lyon an hour and a half to drive to Providence, Rhode Island. It took another twenty minutes to back-track to suburban Cranston where Carillo lived. It was dusk when he arrived at 112 Hutchinson Street, which was a modest stucco house on a quiet thoroughfare not far from Roger Williams Park. Except for minor variations in their tiny front yards, or the addition of an upper-story window dormer, the houses on the street were nearly identical. Constructed on a narrow lot and separated from its neighbor by a concrete drive that led back to a small garage, number 112 had a ceramic pink flamingo standing in a small concrete pool in its minuscule front lawn.

Lyon walked down the short walk and rang the door chime. The first bars of "Ave Maria" echoed through the house interior. When the music-chimes stopped, he rang for an encore. The door was finally opened on the third rendition by a portly man with an astounding shock of gray hair who appeared to be in his late sixties. He carried a spatula in one hand and a long-handled fork in the other. His clothing was obscured by a gigantic white butcher's apron with the words "Greatest Granddad in the World" stitched in red script.

He squinted and flicked the fork under Lyon's chin. "You're Wentworth." The fork tines were millimeters from Lyon's breast bone.

Pan's description of the voice had been excellent, it had a definite guttural quality. "I called about a certain obligation of Mr. Turman's."

The fork waved toward the rear of the house. "In the cellar." Without waiting for a reply, Carillo turned and left Lyon to follow. They passed through the living room where a picture of another flamingo was mounted over the fireplace in a mirrored frame. Identically upholstered furniture was carefully arranged throughout the immaculate room and protected by clear plastic coverings. They went through the kitchen, with its highly waxed floor, and down cellar steps into a family room.

"Mr. Carillo, there's something I should tell you about Dalton Turman," Lyon said.

Carillo, who had crossed to a small kitchen area in the rear of the room turned and waved his utensils at Lyon. "The money. Put the money on the table and we forget about Turman."

"I don't have the money," Lyon said.

Carillo advanced on Lyon with the fork held before him like a lance. Again the tines flicked at Lyon's shirtfront. "You didn't bring money because you don't got no money. I know who you are, just like I know Turman is running."

"Do you know where he is?"

"Not yet. I must do the sausages and peppers." He busied himself at a frying pan on the small stove. "My daughter does not like peppers and sausage to cook in her kitchen. Smells, she says. Of course they smell. They should smell. My daughter is a very good housekeeper. Very neat. Very worried about odors."

"Can we talk privately here? I'm not wired," Lyon said.

Carillo glared at him, waved his spatula in the air and rolled his eyes. "Wired? If you had an electronic transmitter on your person my antisurveillance devices would have sounded an alarm. Why would a provider of venture capital like myself worry about such things?"

"You obviously don't since you phoned him from here," Lyon said.

"Checking up on my money, nothing much illegal. You got to understand they do not watch me like they did. I am what you call semiretired. A little bank for the books, a little loan here and there, a little extortion to keep my hand in. The Feds, all they think about today is drug busts."

"I'm going, Poobah," an adolescent girl with a cream complexion and jet-black hair said from midway down the stairs.

Carillo turned to face her with a broad smile. "Ah, Maria, you are beautiful tonight, but you wear pants on a date?"

"These are designer jeans, Poobah, everyone wears them."

"Everyone, yes. Who are you going with?"

"Jimmie Regan is taking me to the drive-in. We won't be late."

"Be home at eleven."

"Everyone else stays out until midnight."

"Eleven-thirty," Carillo said with a smile. He looked over at Lyon. "See how my granddaughter twists her Poobah around her little finger."

"Bye." The girl scooted up the stairs and a moment later they heard the front door slam.

Carillo handed the spatula to Lyon. "Watch the sausage." Without waiting for a response he dialed the phone. "Regan, Angie Carillo. Your son Jimmie is taking my beloved granddaughter to the movies tonight. I would consider it a favor if he was respectful to her. She has great meaning to me. Thank you." He hung up and resumed his cooking chores. "Regan knows me. I am sure his son will be nice to Maria." He served two plates of sausage and peppers. "It is a great burden to me now that Maria's father is gone. It is very hard to watch after children in these times."

"Divorce is always difficult on kids."

"Eat while we talk. Not divorce. It was a question of firepower. Handguns are useless against automatic weapons and I am afraid that the Colombians have adopted modern technology far quicker than us. Sausages are good, yes? It is important that they have natural casings."

"You seem to know something about me," Lyon said. The food was highly spiced and he reached for the red wine Carillo had set on the table.

"It is important that good sausage be cooked in olive oil that is virgin first press. When you called, I called friends in Hartford who accommodate me. Tell your wife the governor is trying to compromise her."

"Does your knowledge extend to where Dalton is?"

"Let us say we are interested in his journey. We have arranged our own, shall we say, investigators. It would seem that Mr. Turman has decided to take an ocean voyage with large sums of money, some of which, unfortunately, seems to be ours."

"He doesn't seem to be on the ocean. In fact, he doesn't seem to be anywhere."

"He is a very bright man. Once he was able to follow me to a regional meeting with some of my pisanos. It was a quiet house in the country until Turman arranged secret loud speakers and tapes of gunfire." Carillo made an expansive gesture with his knife and nearly knocked over the wine. "Voices called out 'G Men' and that sort of thing. My pisanos were not amused. It was the first time since Tony Anastasia that four contracts were issued simultaneously on the same man. It required much persuasion on my part to get him off with a broken arm."

"Perhaps someone went ahead on his own," Lyon said.
"The families do not kill prominent people anymore, Mr. Wentworth. Only the new immigrants, like the Colombians, do things like that. If we are displeased with someone, we manage to make their lives unpleasant. Drugs are mysteriously found in unlikely places. Wives are seduced by attractive young men, husbands are compromised in many ways, businesses have unexpected difficulties. Who would do business with us if on default they were taken for a walk on Narragansett Bay? Those days are over."

"How about late-night phone calls and a long-range rifle shot at people sitting on a houseboat?"

Carillo shrugged and consumed a whole sausage in one bite. "That is normal business. And the shot did miss everyone, did it not?"

"You practically perform a civic duty," Lyon said.

"The older families are becoming conservative. We have discovered where the real power is. We know that the well-laundered CD is more powerful than an Uzi, that a line of credit is worth ten soldiers in the street. Real estate, a nice business with cash flow, that is for the older men. Leave the machine guns to the Colombians. We have money now, and it is good money for Maria, and it will be old money for Maria's children, as good as any old New England money that got its start in the slave trade."

"It would seem to me that Dalton Turman has a chunk of that laundered money with him."

"If we find him, he will return it. If you or the police find him, he will also return it. We cannot lose."

"Poobah, I hate you!"

Maria was halfway down the stairs clutching the rail with both hands as tears streamed down her cheeks. Angie Carillo's face darkened as he folded his napkin and stood. "The boy will pay for this."

"Pay for what!" she screamed at her grandfather. "He never touched me. We were at the drive-in and he had his arm around me and we were getting ready to . . . when his father drove in and practically hit us. Mr. Regan pulled Jimmie out of the car and whispered to him. When Jimmie came back he sat against the door. Then he said he felt sick and drove me home at about ninety miles an hour. I could die! You do this all the time, Poobah. How am I ever going to make out?" She ran back up the stairs.

Carillo began to slowly gather the empty plates. "It is the young. There is no satisfying them."

7 When Lyon left 112 Hutchinson Street in Cranston, Rhode Island, he immediately knew that crime was rampant in the country, and that lawlessness ruled the land like the riders of the Apocalypse.

His car had been stolen. The parking space directly in front of the home of one of the most senior mafia leaders in New England had provided no protection.

A tan Ford with an accordion-shaped right fender, eased from the driveway of a vacant house across the street. It slowed to a stop and Rocco reached across the seat and flipped open the door on the passenger's side. "In," he commanded.

Lyon did as instructed. "You had my car driven home?"

"Yep." Rocco threw the car in gear and accelerated as he cornered a curve dangerously. "I told you no Rhode Island."

"He doesn't seem like a vicious man, and he's very concerned about his granddaughter's chastity."

"And of course he fed you?"

"Some excellent sausage and peppers. I've got to remember the way he prepared them."

"For Christ sake, Lyon, didn't you ever hear of the banality of evil?"

"Most street cops I know aren't aware of Hannah Arendt."

"You don't know any street cops except me."

"What help could you have been to me sitting in a car across the street?"

"He wouldn't have burned you in his own house, and I wasn't about to let them take you on any trips in car trunks. Did you find out anything?"

"His people are the ones who took the shot at the houseboat, but I don't think they did anything to Dalton except try to frighten him. As long as they thought the construction job was doing well, they expected to get their money back. They would have nothing to gain by taking Dalton and the boat."

Rocco increased the speed of the car as a response to his mood. "God, you're naive. They had a million-plus reasons to do something to Dalton, and the money was probably hidden somewhere on that damn boat."

There was a tone of resignation in Bea's voice as she stood in the doorway of the cellar recreation room. "When the maps go on the Ping-Pong table and he breaks out the magnifying glass, I know we're in trouble."

"Because of the overlaps on some of our flights, the

map is actually larger than you requested," Gary Dorset said as he kicked the Ping-Pong net further under the table.

"It's just fine, Gary," Lyon said as he finished securing the last of the aerial-photograph strips in place. He stepped back from the table to look at the complete composite that included the banks of the Connecticut River from mid-Massachusetts to the Atlantic Ocean. It also included the Connecticut shoreline from Bridgeport to the Rhode Island border and the islands in that area.

Bea peered over the table. "It's a little late to mention it, but we could have bought a map of the same area for fifty cents at the Mobil station."

"Wouldn't be the same," Lyon said as he realigned one of the strips. "Is Pan around?"

"She went back to the resort to get more of her things. I think she's moved in permanently."

"Do you get along with her?" Lyon asked.

Bea thought a moment before replying. "That depends. It's like living with a combination of Doris Day and Lucrezia Borgia. When you ask her something, you're either going to get a burst of 'Que Serra Serra' or the poisoned ring. You can never tell."

"I found that duality too," Lyon said as he bent over the table with his magnifying glass to minutely examine a portion of the shoreline.

"Well, I'm off," Bea said without receiving any response. "I'll be late for dinner, as I'm having an affair with the Governor."

"Don't hurry," Lyon said as he inched further over the map with his eyes inches from the photographs.

"We'll probably make love in the well of the Senate," Bea said.

"Drive carefully," Lyon said.

*   *   *

He'd have to stop. After several hours of painstaking searching, his senses had dulled and become unresponsive. He hadn't found what he was looking for.

Lyon knew that the *Mississippi* was basically an unseaworthy vessel. It might be capable of making short hops between Caribbean Islands during fair weather, or it could safely navigate the inland waterway, but the craft's blunt lines and small draft made lengthy sea voyages not only hazardous, but nearly suicidal. His theory required the houseboat to still be in the vicinity of the Connecticut River. The expensive aerial map he'd prepared had not revealed what it should have revealed.

There was something he wasn't seeing. His knowledge of the state and shore had been confirmed by the aerial pictures, but there was still something he had either missed or hadn't viewed properly.

Sawhorses were placed on either side of the access road leading to the Pincus Resort. A two-by-four stretched between them carried a ROAD CLOSED sign. Lyon removed the barrier and drove into the complex.

In the few days since Dalton's disappearance, decay had already taken root at the unfinished project. Construction equipment had been abandoned in the middle of tasks, and building materials appeared as if they had been haphazardly dropped by departing workmen at a prearranged signal. The area had a general aura of desolation.

The dusty station wagon with the Pranko Construction Company logo on its sides was parked in front of a small building near what was to have been the recreation center. Lyon parked behind the wagon and entered the building. The reception area was deserted, as were the sales closing rooms and front offices. Empty desks and hanging wires marked where typewriters, copying machines, and other office equipment had once stood.

Two men were in small offices at the rear of the building. Sam, the construction foreman, was surrounded by dozens of phone books and had a telephone pressed to his ear. "A houseboat that's nearly eighty feet long called the *Mississippi* . . . any houseboats called anything . . . okay, thanks." He slammed down the receiver. "So much for New Jersey, now I start on Delaware."

"You're calling all the marinas on the Eastern seaboard?" Lyon asked in amazement.

"Damn right! He can't hide that tub forever. He has to stop somewhere for gas and supplies, and when he does, I'll find him."

"The Coast Guard has already tried," Lyon said.

"They don't have a stake in this like I do." He began to dial another number. "Can't talk now. Got to keep calling until the phone company finds out what's going on and cuts off our lines . . . Hello, Blue Point Marina? I'm calling . . ."

Lyon went into the office next door. He recognized the man behind the desk as Dalton's partner and financial officer, Randolph Dice. Dice sat behind a desk piled high with ledgers and computer printouts. He held a pocket calculator in one hand and stared blankly off into space until he became aware of Lyon's presence. "If you've come to pick up the computer terminals, you're too late. The bank already grabbed them."

"I'm Wentworth. I was on the *Mississippi* the other day."

"If you're one of Dalton's friends, I don't need to guess why you're here. He borrowed money from you and you want to call in the note."

"I'm trying to find him."

"You are a member of a large but not very exclusive group."

Randolph Dice was a short man bordering on the fat in his early thirties with a squat build. There was a physical softness about him that seemed reflected in the scrubbed pinkness of his complexion, flabby facial features, and a body that must have taken great pains to avoid all physical exertion.

"Do you have any ideas where he might be?" Lyon asked.

"If I did, I would gladly hire someone to annihilate him. Let me tell you something, Wentworth. I left an extremely prestigious position with a management consulting firm to join this organization. I had this mistaken idea that I wanted to become a bold, young entrepreneur. Instead, I am rapidly becoming a bankrupt, aging accountant." He threw a ledger across the room and let it clatter against the wall. "And I got an MBA from Harvard for this?"

"That's our record," Lyon said automatically.

"I beg your pardon?"

"An unimportant passing thought," Lyon said. For years he and Bea had kept a tally on how quickly it took a Harvard graduate to announce his or her alma mater. Randolph Dice now held the record. "How much is missing?"

"About a million-two-plus, as best I can reconstruct it so far, but I'm not finished yet."

"I still don't understand how he got all that cash from a company in financial trouble."

"In any multimillion dollar operation there are numerous accounts, escrows, bank floats, compensating balances, and other types of money available to an unscrupulous and clever manipulator. The only difficulty is that most of that money does not belong to us. The bankruptcy court is going to bury us."

"And you weren't aware of any of this?"

"Of excessive spending and poor cash control, yes. Massive fraud, no. He made false entries, ran the money through different accounts and finally converted it to cash. How the hell can I explain that to the authorities? Sam and I are going to look like fools at best, co-conspirators at worst. In addition, we're going to lose all our personal assets."

"You voluntarily put those assets on the line," Lyon said, "because you thought this project would make money."

"It could have."

"Then why did Dalton steal from it and run with less than he could have made legitimately?"

Randolph Dice put both hands to his head and slowly rocked back and forth. "I don't know. If I understood, I might know a lot of other things."

"What happens if he's found dead without the cash?"

Dice's hands dropped away from his face as he looked at Lyon with a new antagonism. "In that instance, I would be a murder suspect."

"Who else could have known about the missing cash at the time Dalton disappeared?"

"Sam, of course. Dalton's wife, Pandora, could have known. Then there was talk that Dalton and Katrina Loops had a thing going. She might have known. If Katrina knew, and since she's involved with Bobby Douglas, he might have known."

Looking out the window, Lyon saw a tow truck lifting the front end of the Pranko Construction Company station wagon. "Someone seems to be interfering with your automobile," he said.

Dice took a disinterested glance. "They're repossessing it, like everything else around here."

"What are your plans?" Lyon asked.

"I don't have any choice, Mr. Wentworth. Dalton's actions have sentenced me to an indeterminate sentence tied to this project until some court, months or years from now, lets me go."

"I'd like to talk to Bobby Douglas," Lyon said.

Dice's short burst of laughter was like the double snap of a clapboard. "That rat was the first to leave this sinking sandpile. He was gone the morning after Dalton's disappearing act. There's no one left out here except Kat Loops, who we let occupy one of the cottages."

"She's still waiting for her boyfriend who ain't never coming back," Sam said from the doorway.

Dice's face brightened for the first time. "You found out something?"

"Damn right! I just got off the phone with the Blue Bay Marina in Rehoboth Beach, Delaware. They didn't know from nothing about the *Mississippi,* but thought it funny that a guy was there for two days asking the same questions. They said he was good looking and seemed to know boats. He had a great suntan and walked with a limp. Guess who?"

"What in hell is Bobby doing in Delaware?" Dice said.

"Because," Sam continued, "from the way he talked to the marina people he expected the *Mississippi* to be there. The tennis-playing bastard intended to meet Dalton in Delaware."

"Get the police on the phone," Dice snapped.

"You got it!" Sam snatched the telephone from its cradle and began to dial.

Lyon turned to leave. "By the way," he said to Dice. "When you boarded the *Mississippi* the other day you were quite angry until Dalton talked to you. What did he say?"

"Captain Norbert, please," Sam said over the phone as he looked at Dice with interest.

Lyon had often heard the phrase "all the color drain-ing," but had never before actually witnessed anyone turn instantly pale. Dice's eyes widened, and he gulped air as if hyperventilating.

"What in the hell did he say to you?" Sam demanded.

"Nothing," Dice finally articulated.

Sam's eyes locked with Lyon's. "That sounds like a hell of a powerful nothing, if you ask me."

"It's not important," Dice said as he stumbled around his desk and dashed for the hall and a small bathroom next door.

"I think someone has something on someone." Sam said. "Hello, Captain Norbert. We got a line on the bas-tard."

He found Katrina Loops sunbathing on the narrow beach just beyond the seawall. She lay facedown on a large beach towel with a small towel over her round bot-tom. She seemed to stretch from the high-water mark to the seawall. A paperback novel lay near her right hand, a small Thermos jug by the left. He noticed that there wasn't any bra strap crossing her bare back, and that gave him a strong suspicion that there was little if anything but Katrina under the small towel that covered her rear.

She had obviously fallen asleep in the warm sun, and this presented a problem of decorum. How do you po-litely awaken a nearly naked lady without causing her movements to throw off the single modest covering she wore? He decided that no matter how he approached the problem, there was going to be a moment or two when his lascivious thoughts were apparent. He bent down and gently shook her arm.

"Katrina. It's Lyon Wentworth."

She didn't respond, but his modest shaking movement caused the towel to slowly slide onto the sand. She lay nude before him and he hastily stood and turned away. The waters of the Sound were a grayish blue with Long Island's low profile in the distance. Something was wrong.

Something was drastically wrong.

He turned and knelt. He felt her wrist and then his fingers searched for the carotid artery. He grasped her shoulder and slowly turned her over. Her eyes were wide open and the pupils were fixed as her head lolled loosely to the side. Katrina Loops was quite dead.

Lyon recoiled from the obscenity of death. He had seen its face many times, in different places and guises, but each time it seemed uniquely and horribly fresh. A living personality had been obliterated and reduced to a mass of dying cells.

A thin ribbon of blood had oozed from a narrow slit between her breasts. It seemed apparent that she had been stabbed with a thin-bladed knife that had pierced the sternum and entered the myocardium to cause instant death.

He turned away and walked slowly back to the office, where he found Sam and Randy in whispered consultation. They looked up with annoyance at his intrusion.

"I think you had better get Captain Norbert back on the phone," Lyon said.

The Pincus Resort was located in the small town of Eastbrook, which did not have its own full-time police force. Police services were provided by a part-time constabulary and a resident state trooper with backup from the local barracks. This meant that Captain Norbert and his men descended on the scene in large numbers.

Lyon sat on the seawall fifty yards down from the body. Pan Turman sat by his side and shivered in the warm sun. Police cruisers, official vans, and an ambulance speckled the lawns. A bevy of officers and technicians surrounded the body and spoke in hushed tones.

"She must have family somewhere," Pan said. "Later, I'll see if I can find her personnel file and see who it lists so I can phone them. She was such a beautiful woman. Large, but put together well with a marvelous figure. She was a great salesperson and sold more units than anyone else, but there is one little small, tiny thing about it all."

Lyon looked at her. "What's that?"

Pan pulled his head down to her lips with both hands and whispered in a deep voice. "The wicked witch is dead. The bitchy witch is dead, and am I glad."

Lyon recoiled from her and looked into her sparkling eyes. "You don't mean that."

"I knew about them from the start, you know. Oh, they thought they were so smart about it, and she even took up with Bobby to throw me off the track, but I knew. I knew from the first time they did it together, and now she'll never screw anybody ever again."

He inched along the seawall away from her, but she grasped both his hands in hers and held him. He wondered if the specks in her eyes were madness or reflected ocean light, or was her naiveté such that she didn't properly assess what she was really saying? Was this slight woman strong enough to attack and pierce the breastbone of a far larger woman with one thrust of the knife? "You don't mean what you're saying, Pan," he finally said.

Her head tilted as she smiled with a childlike radiance. "Oh, silly, of course I didn't kill her. I just meant that it doesn't break me up. I will send lots of nice flowers to her family. Will we have to stay around here much longer?"

"They're going to want statements from both of us," Lyon answered.

"Well, there's nothing I can tell them, except that I've been staying at your house, and when I came out here this morning I think Katrina purposely avoided me."

"You know, Pan, they'll speak to you today and then check and cross-check until they're satisfied that you've told them everything."

She hugged her shoulders as if a dank breeze had blown in from the sea. "They'll have lots of questions." It was a statement.

"A great many," Lyon answered softly. "They're going to want to know if you were aware that Dalton had a great deal of money converted into cash."

"I knew he had all that money, but he told me that he needed cash to pay off that man who called in the night. They'll find out about Katrina and Dalton, won't they?"

"Yes."

Captain Norbert stalked toward them. He glowered at Lyon. "I understand that you found the body? Let me ask you something, Wentworth. How do you manage to find the time to stumble over half the murder victims in my jurisdiction?"

"I think it has something to do with my karma, Captain."

"It's because of all the time you have on your hands. Why don't you get a real job like the rest of us?"

"Is this employment counseling time, or are you conducting an investigation?"

"I'll get your statement later." He shifted his attention to Pan Turman and as he did his manner changed to that of the polite but firm civil servant. "We'd like your permission to search the premises including all the motor vehicles. We could get a court order, but it would save time if you allowed it."

"Sure," Pan said as she pointed across the compound. "That cottage over there is where I stayed before I went to the Wentworths'. The one next to it was Katrina's. The cars are all parked up in the lot."

Captain Norbert gave her a half-salute and walked away to give orders to a phalanx of patrolmen and detectives.

"What in the hell's going on?" Bobby Douglas limped across the grass toward them.

"When did you get back?" Lyon asked.

"I just pulled into the parking lot and a dozen troopers crawled all over me. What happened? Did they find Dalton's body?"

"Kat's been killed," Pan said. "She was on the beach where someone stabbed her."

"Katrina dead?" Douglas looked stricken, and as if to punctuate his feelings, ambulance attendants zippered a body bag shut, levered it on a gurney, and pushed it to a waiting ambulance. The vehicle's doors closed and it pulled slowly away from the resort. Douglas sank slowly to a seat on the seawall.

"What were you doing at a marina in Delaware?" Lyon asked.

Douglas looked up at Lyon as the shutters behind his eyes flicked open and shut several times while he decided what to answer. He finally spoke in a hesitant manner with long pauses. "I thought Dalton would be down there. That was sort of the original plan."

"What plan?" Lyon asked.

"The way he had it set up, I was the one supposed to take the boat, and he was to meet me at the marina. We were to sail south and then make a run for one of the Bahamas."

"With the cash aboard?"

"He never said exactly, but that's the way I figured it. When he and the boat were gone, I thought it was the same plan in reverse, and that he'd want me to meet him. He never showed. I don't think he made it out of the river."

"What did Katrina know?"

Douglas shrugged. "Who knows? Kat would tell you what she wanted you to know she knew."

"You, Douglas." Captain Norbert was back and held an acetate evidence bag in his hand.

Bobby didn't look up at him. "Yeah."

"The red eighty-four Ford in the lot yours?"

"Mine and the bank's."

"This yours?" Norbert shoved the evidence bag at him. "We found it under the seat of your car." The bag held a yellow spring knife with a narrow, stained blade.

"Looks like one I have."

"Forensic will tell us for sure, but it looks like we got blood on your knife, boy."

Douglas shifted uneasily. "I might have cut myself. I eat lots of fruit."

"During our investigation of Turman's disappearance, we ran a make on you, Douglas. We know you had a drug bust in Florida."

"For carrying half an ounce of grass, for Chrissake!" Bobby said. "It musta been a slow day for cops that afternoon."

"Seems there were going to be more slow days for you after your girl ran away with Turman and his money," Norbert said. "Or did you take care of that little detail too?"

"Wait a goddamn minute!" Douglas took a menacing step toward Norbert until the police officer grasped the butt of the weapon holstered at his waist. "I spent sixty days in the can in Florida, and I won't go through that again."

"You have the right to remain silent . . ." Norbert began in a monotone.

"Bullshit!" Douglas ran toward the parking lot. His limping stride slowed him somewhat, but his powerful legs still propelled him rapidly toward the red car at the edge of the lot.

Norbert dropped the evidence bag and held his service

revolver in his right hand as his left braced the wrist. He began to lead the barrel after the running man. "Stop! I order you to stop."

Lyon glanced at Norbert's aim expecting to see the revolver's barrel pointed high in a warning shot. The captain had assumed a marksman's stance and was still leading the running man with care. It was going to be a carefully aimed, if not fatal, shot.

"No!" Lyon yelled as the palm of one hand lashed out and struck the police officer in the larynx while the other wrenched the pistol from the captain's hand.

Norbert staggered backward clutching his throat. He pointed at the running man and choked out, "Get him!"

On the far side of the seawall, a State Police officer raised the M-16 he had cradled over his arm and took aim as Bobby Douglas reached for his car door.

Lyon fired Norbert's weapon directly at the officer pointing the rifle.

Lyon hadn't realized before that most state cops carried blackjacks in their back pockets. His fresh bruises, bloodied nose, and other assorted aches were proof of this new knowledge. The massive shooting pains in his head were of some minor help in that they made him forget lesser pains in other parts of his anatomy.

After he had fired at the officer sighting the rifle, state cops had descended on him from all directions in massive numbers. They might have killed him if Norbert hadn't recovered sufficiently to stop the mayhem. Lyon would always be convinced that the State Police captain let the beating continue for a minute or two longer than necessary.

The small holding cell at the barracks didn't help his disposition. They had laughed when he'd asked for his single phone call, and they hadn't bothered to book, photograph, or fingerprint him. He had been dragged unceremoniously from the cruiser, through the communications room, and dumped on the floor of the cell. The door had slammed with a note of finality.

No one had died, and that was some consolation for the beating. Before he lost consciousness from the attack by the irate troopers, he had seen Douglas taken into custody and the officer he had shot hobble toward a cruiser using his rifle as a crutch. After that, things began to get hazy.

He swung his legs from the bunk and staggered over to a plumbing fixture that contained a toilet, sink, and built-in mirror all in one unit. His face, reflected in the stainless steel, verified visually how he felt physically. The knowledge that he would probably look worse tomorrow didn't help.

All that the narrow cell contained was the plumbing fixture and the bunk. Stools, desks, lamps, and reading matter were evidently not provided to the occupants of holding cells. He assumed that the purpose of this was to make the prisoner contemplate his sins. He flopped back on the bunk and laced his hands behind his head, but even that simple gesture shot tentacles of pain along his arms.

It was time to go to another place. He had an eclectic memory able to transform past experiences and images into a vivid near-reality. It was a question of roaming through memories and selecting. He decided to view a river trip he and his father had taken on his fourteenth birthday. It had been a Technicolor day, with a warm but not burning sun and a moderate breeze from the north. They had launched the twenty-one-foot sailboat into the

Connecticut River at East Hartford. Spring freshets had brimmed the river and the current was brisk. Wind stiffened the sails as they turned into the main channel.

He meticulously reconstructed the exact details of the trip downriver. The day's sights were as vivid now as they had been during that day decades ago, but his father's facial features were beginning to blur, and he wondered why that seemed to happen as the years progressed.

They sailed to the sea by following the river's meandering course as it wandered toward the Sound. They passed Middleburg, where years later he would teach at the University. They drifted past the promontory where he now lived, and finally reached the mouth of the river. They slept on the boat that night, and at dawn were under sail again. They wandered in and out of channels that separated the small islands that occasionally clustered near the shore. They tacked by the lee side of Duck Island and ran before a stiff wind that pushed them rapidly past Red Deer Island, which even then was deserted. They slept that night in a safe anchorage protected by the Thimble Islands.

The memory covered nearly the identical area that Lyon had Dorset map with his aerial photographs. The whole shore was more densely populated now, and the configurations of some land had changed due to water erosion or storms. The house on Red Deer Island had been destroyed by a hurricane last year, and Duck Island had completely disappeared underwater.

Lyon's eyes snapped open to immediately destroy the phantom sailing trip. He stared at the ceiling a moment before catapulting from the bunk to grab the bars on the cell door. "Get me out of here!" His voice echoed in the narrow concrete hallway. "Damn it! Let me out of here!"

"Shut up!" a voice from another cell yelled back. "We're trying to sleep."

"Psycho time," another voice added.

The chant repeating Lyon's demand began at the cell at the end of the corridor and was quickly taken up by all the prisoners until the din of "Let us out" became ear shattering.

The single state trooper who entered the hall and growled for quiet was shouted down and soon retreated for reinforcements. Captain Norbert, wearing a bandage around his throat, appeared in the hall flanked by four large troopers. His voice boomed above the din. "Who started this?"

"The guy in the cell at the end," someone answered.

"Wentworth!" Captain Norbert's voice cracked. "You son of a bitch!"

Rocco Herbert followed the troopers who followed Norbert as he stalked toward Lyon's cell. "Leave him alone, Norbie," Rocco said.

"Yeah, wait until I finish telling you what this bastard did." He stopped in front of Lyon and poked an accusing finger through the bars. "Assault, attempted murder, and resisting arrest. And those are just for openers. It's going to be hard time for you, Wentworth."

Rocco shoved his way to the cell door and looked in at Lyon with horror. "You beat the shit out of him," he said in a low voice. "You worked him over."

"Boy, did we," one of the flanking troopers said. "After he shot MacIntire in the foot, we were all over his ass."

Rocco's fist tore into the trooper's abdomen. When the patrolman grunted and bent forward, Rocco's knee snapped into his chin and flipped him backward. He grabbed Norbert's uniform lapels with one hand while the other slapped the captain repeatedly across the face.

Another trooper began rapid kidney punches into Rocco's side, while two others struggled in the narrow space to reach their blackjacks.

Based on his own recent experience, Lyon estimated that subduing Rocco was going to be at least a six-man job. The hallway was going to get very crowded.

Bea stood in front of the cell with a police report in her hand. She shook her head as she looked in at the two quiet men locked inside. "You gave Captain Norbert a ka-rate chop to the throat? And what's this larceny charge?"

"I think that's for stealing his pistol," Lyon said.

"And Rocco assaulted seven state troopers?"

"I swear, Bea, I only counted six."

She looked at the list again. "Lyon shot a state trooper in the foot? This is ridiculous. There's a combined total of sixteen charges against you two."

Captain Norbert stood behind Bea and fingered the new bandage on his forehead. "I think we're talking five to seven in max security here. The boys up there hate cops, it's going to be hard time for Rocco."

"Your sister is going to be very pissed when she finds out you busted me," Rocco said.

Bea leaned dejectedly against the wall. "This whole mat-ter is most unfortunate for all of us, and means that a great many careers are going down the drain. One of the things I've based my political career on is strict gun-control legislation." She looked down at the police report. "And yet my husband is arrested for unlawful possession of a firearm and attempted murder. Rocco certainly can't remain police chief when he's in jail for assaulting eight state troopers."

"Six," Rocco insisted.

"Seven," Norbert corrected.

"I'm sure you'll survive somehow, Captain, but the town cops in this state won't be very happy with you for failing to respect a badge, particularly the one worn by the newly elected president of the state's Police Chiefs' Association."

"I haven't seen you since that election, Rocco," Norbert said. "Congratulations."

"Thanks."

Bea sighed. "As usual, the only one to come out of this mess whole will be Lyon. He can write books anywhere, and the more maximum the security the more time he'll have to write. His publishers will probably ask him to do a well-paid exposé of the state police. Children's-book writers can't go around shooting policemen, but he can use a pseudonym."

"Who was shot?" Norbert said as he took the report from Bea's hand, ripped it up, and stuffed it into his pocket. He unlocked the cell door. "I want to thank Chief Herbert for coming down here today to give my men a valuable lesson in unarmed combat. He grabbed Lyon's head harshly with both hands and whispered into his ear. "We have a phrase for it, Wentworth. It's called 'lost in society.' That's for guys like you who we know are bad guys, and who know that we know, but who we got to use for one reason or another. We let them go, like I am today, but you get lost. You don't even spit on the sidewalks. You don't even rip a warning label off a bed mattress. You just disappear. You get lost. And you better not be found around any more dead people unless it's a state funeral."

Lyon stepped away from the angry State Police officer. "I understand."

Bea shook Norbert's hand. "Just this morning I was telling the Commissioner what a fine job you do in this part of the state, Captain."

"Thank you, Senator." He clapped Rocco on the back. "We're having a barbecue on Sunday. You and Martha will come, of course?"

"Naturally," Rocco replied.

As they started to leave the cell block Norbert gestured to a middle cell. Bobby Douglas sat dejectedly on the edge of the bunk with his hands hanging between his knees. "Hey, Douglas. The lab called with their report, that *is* the victim's blood on your knife. You'll be arraigned in the morning."

Lyon waved the others on and went over to Bobby's cell. He heard Norbert whisper a comment to Bea in the hall. "I don't understand how a nice lady like you lives with a guy like that, Senator. Excuse me, I must tell MacIntire that he's a corporal. That ought to improve his foot."

Bobby looked up and forced a smile. "That was one hell of a fight in there. I wish I coulda helped you guys."

"Did you kill her, Bobby?"

"I swear to God, I didn't, Mr. Wentworth. I hadn't seen my knife in days. I don't know how it got blood on it."

"When was the last time you saw Dalton?"

"When I left the *Mississippi* with you. Right after we docked on the river across from your place."

"Who would want to kill Katrina?"

"I think she was becoming a pain in the butt to Dalton. If he were around, he'd be on my list, but if not him, maybe his wife, Pan. Maybe she knew something she wasn't supposed to know. I only know I didn't kill her."

"None of us in here did nuthin'," the voice from the next cell said. "We're like victims of circumstances."

There was a lot of laughing as Lyon left the cell block.

It was probably because Bea was still treating them as two recalcitrant young boys that made Rocco insist on stopping at Sarge's Place. Renfroe stuffed his dirty bar rag under the counter as they entered.

"What the hell happened, Captain? I ain't seen you beat

up so bad since the time you and me took on the cops in Phenix City outside of Benning."

"They tell me I gave a class in unarmed combat. Set us up, Sarge."

Bea followed them in after parking the car. She was halfway to the table when Sarge caught up to her. His large ham-hand came down in an arcing sweep that caught her flat across the rear and staggered her forward a few feet.

"How are you, babe? I ain't seen you in a while, Senator."

"I think there's probably a reason for that, Sarge," Bea answered.

Renfroe gave her a bear hug. "You can put your shoes under my bunk anytime, honey."

"You don't go to bed, Sarge, you pass out. How about a pink lady."

"You don't drink those things," Lyon said as she sat down.

"I like to make Sarge's life difficult."

"Bobby tells me he didn't kill Katrina," Lyon said.

"Bull diddle!" Rocco said. "He was jumping her, he knew that Dalton had money on the boat, the knife is his, he was at the resort, and he's got priors. Norbie and the state's attorney will have him begging for murder two in a couple of days."

"What about Dalton as the killer?" Bea suggested.

"He's dead," Lyon said positively.

"Like he was dead in that coffin in our living room. Come on, Went," Bea said. "He found out his mistress was two-timing him and so he got rid of her and her lover."

"Where's the *Mississippi?*" Rocco asked. "A joke is one thing, an impossibility another."

"He sank it in the ocean," Bea said with finality.

"How did he get it out there past the bridges, the Army Corps of Engineers, and the Coast Guard?"

"I'm working on that," Bea said.

"I think he was killed, either for the cash he had on the boat or for other reasons." Lyon began to tick suspects off his fingers. "There's the Rhode Island contingent that weren't pleased with him. Randy Dice blames all his problems on Dalton, and Sam Idelweise certainly isn't happy."

"Don't forget Miss Conviviality," Bea said. "There are things about her that I'm only beginning to suspect."

Sarge served Lyon's sherry, Rocco's vodka, and a third drink of strange coloration. Bea shook her head.

"You know, one day one of us is going to get a phone call from Rio and there's going to be a strange laugh and guess who?"

"I think not," Lyon said.

"I have to go to work," Bea said. "Lyon will not make any airplane or balloon trips. He will not pass 'go.' He will go home and write great literature, and he will give me half his drink, because I can't take Sarge's latest potion."

No airplane or balloon trips, Lyon thought to himself as he walked out to their barn at Nutmeg Hill. She hadn't mentioned anything about boats. He was convinced that his theory concerning the location of the *Mississippi* was the only remaining possibility. However, it was so outlandish that he was embarrassed to bring it to the police's or his wife's attention until he had verified it.

It took nearly an hour of hard work in the barn to move balloon equipment, lawn tools, and cartons of unknown contents that blocked access to the fourteen-foot runabout. It had been three years since the boat had been used, and in the interim a family of some sort of rodentia had obviously utilized it as a rat-staging area. It took another hour to clean the boat, mount it on its trailer, and attach the outboard to the rear transom. The engine had to be oiled and the carburetor adjusted until it ran without ragged bursts of exhaust.

He searched through the balloon gondola for other equipment and attached a flat, waist life belt with a small CO_2 cartridge for inflation, under his sport shirt. A hunting vest with its numerous pockets and pouches was useful for holding other items. He clipped a flashlight to a ring on the vest, while a compass and map went into another pocket. A Swiss Army knife, a camera with flash attachment, and a candy bar filled the game pouch at the rear of the vest. He put a short crowbar into the boat along with a pair of binoculars.

He had everything he needed except for the ignition keys to the station wagon that was to pull the runabout to the mouth of the river. He hurried back to the kitchen where their duplicate keys hung on a board. There was a neatly printed note where they should have been: "Did I neglect to mention car trips?"

"You look mad as a hornet," Pan said from the kitchen doorway.

"I need to go somewhere in the wagon and can't find the car keys and my divorce is going to be expensive." It was even worse—he could see the Wobblies standing in his study doorway beckoning to him.

"I saw you hook up the boat to the station wagon. Can I go with you?"

"I'd rather go alone, if I *were* going."

"Why don't you hot-wire it?"

"I don't know how."

"I'll show you. When you grow up in a small Southern town like I did, you learn that boys are only interested in two things, and the second is cars."

He drove the secondary highway that ran most nearly parallel to the river until he reached its mouth near the railroad bridge. He parked the station wagon at a state boat-launching area almost directly underneath the bridge and uncoupled the trailer. Holding tightly to the trailer's tongue, he backed it down the ramp until the boat floated free. He pulled the start rope on the outboard until the engine kicked into life. He threw the motor in gear, gave a hard right to the rudder, and sailed under the railroad bridge and out past the point into the Sound.

It took over an hour for the small outboard to reach a position that was five hundred yards off Red Deer Island. He put the motor in neutral and let the boat drift as he lifted the binoculars and swept the terrain of the small islet.

It was exactly as he remembered it. It appeared today the same way it had when he sailed here with his father those many years ago. It hadn't changed in fifty years, not since the last occupants of the house boarded the windows and left forever after donating the property to the Audubon Society as a bird sanctuary.

It was the same, and that was the flaw, as he knew that the remains of the house had been demolished during a hurricane a year ago. He focused the glasses on the structure.

The dwelling had been constructed at the edge of what was once a broad beach, but which over the years had eroded into a narrow strip of sand. The structure was covered in vines and brush. The front veranda had crumpled years ago, until only a few posts and rotting boards remained. Planks and sheets of plywood had been nailed across the doors and windows. Because of the way the house was built in relation to the water, only the front and part of one side were visible from any off-island location. Dense foliage obscured the other side and rear.

He let the motorboat drift closer to shore. When the distance had halved, he could see where some of the foliage growing over the building was beginning to brown.

It was dying. He felt he was close to the solution of the boat's disappearance. When he knew what had happened to Dalton, perhaps the murder of Katrina would be explained.

The runabout beached on the narrow strip of sand, and water lapped gently at the edge of his canvas shoes as he stepped ashore and pulled the boat above the high-water mark. He stood before the heavily shuttered house holding the crowbar.

"Like a damn Q-ship," he said aloud. Armed ships of war had often been disguised as cumbersome freighters to lure the enemy. It was time to discover if Dalton had audaciously adapted this concept.

He stepped toward a sealed doorway and inserted the crowbar into a seam and began to pry. He had to pull down with his complete weight before screeching nails signaled the separation of the exterior planking from its interior attachment. He stepped quickly backward as the plank ripped free and fell to the ground.

Instead of peering into the dim musty interior of a sealed house, he faced the sleek side of the houseboat. The exterior of the house was a facade, a cleverly constructed front similar to a movie set. The ground to his right that led toward the water was riffled, as if it had been scoured with tree branches after the *Mississippi* had been winched ashore.

He began to pry other sections away from the building's false exterior, and with each additional piece the pattern became more obvious. The *Mississippi* had slipped its moorings from the dock across from Nutmeg Hill and drifted downstream until its engines could be safely started. They—for Dalton would have needed help—would have taken the craft to a dark and deserted cove where the false panels had been attached.

The blunt lines of the houseboat had been camouflaged

as the squat coastal tanker reported by the second bridge operator. They had sailed the unseaworthy craft out of the river and the few miles to Red Deer Island. Once it had been winched ashore, the disguise panels had been reversed and reset as they had been designed to be, and the boat became the shuttered house.

The flimsy facade would not hold up indefinitely, but would probably go undetected through a summer or more unless discovered by trespassing boys. Dalton, carrying his hoard of cash, had pulled the ultimate prank.

He reached over the houseboat rail and pulled high enough to inch first one leg, then another, over the side so that he could drop to the deck. There was a dank, sweetish odor in the darkened craft. It was a smell of must and dead things. Lyon involuntarily shivered as he unhooked the flashlight from the vest. He switched it on and swiveled the light over the interior. It was as if the craft's short double life had accelerated its deterioration. Brass was smudged, a film of dust and dirt lay across all flat surfaces, and the deck planks were scarred and marred by cuts and scratches. Several of the large windows in the saloon were broken or cracked.

He climbed over stray pieces of equipment and worked his way to the saloon entrance. He had to push aside brush, cushions, and other debris before he could force open the door and step inside.

His light flicked abruptly from side to side as he absorbed the devastation. The once-sumptuous saloon was a shambles. Knife slashes slit cushions, carpeting had been peeled away from the deck, and large swatches of wood paneling had been torn from the bulkheads. Someone had carried out a frantic search without concern for its trail of destruction.

The smell he had noticed on the outside deck was more pronounced in the saloon. He pushed his way past overturned furniture into the dining room where the odor was nearly overpowering.

Dalton Turman was in the master stateroom, and the source of the smell.

His feet dangled a few inches from the deck as he hung by the neck from a rope hooked over a spike driven into the wall. The remains of his clothing hung in long tatters as a result of long knife strokes whose paths streaked his body in tortuous strokes.

Lyon gagged and ran from the stateroom. He was nearly to the saloon door when two men appeared in the entrance. They both wore stocking masks, and the larger one slammed him against the bulkhead with a massive thrust of his shoulders.

"Kill him," the smaller man said.

9

Lyon groaned.

"Idiot!" The voice seemed a thousand miles away. "I told you to kill the son of a bitch."

"Hell, I hit him hard enough. What difference does it make? He's going to drown in a minute and a half."

He frantically groped for coherence, and the voices did seem clearer as the echo effect faded. He forced his eyes open only to look into a black well filled with concentric rings of light that moved toward and past him. He attempted a body orientation in order to establish his physical position. He discovered that his feet were tightly bound at the ankles, and his hands were tied behind his back. He lay facedown on an uneven wooden surface. He

College of the Ouachitas

could feel vibrations sending slight tremors through his body, and there was a pronounced yaw movement. Cool spray sprinkled the back of his neck.

He was in a boat. Judging by the craft's beam and reaction to swells, he assumed it was a small craft propelled by an outboard motor. It was probably his own runabout.

"You know how they float to the surface after a couple of days," the man at the stern said.

"Jesus, I know that," the second man answered. "I got his feet tied to a couple of cement blocks I found out there." He laughed. "He's going to float like a stone."

"Like walking on Narragansett Bay," the first man said and they both laughed.

Their voices were familiar. Lyon turned his head and felt tendrils of pain shoot down his neck and across his shoulders. The light was dim and his eyes were still not focusing enough to allow him to completely make out their features. He could tell that the man nearest the outboard was the larger, and that both of them had discarded their stocking masks.

"Would you guys consider merely maiming me?" Lyon said.

The man at the tiller laughed. "Well, we could rip your tongue out."

"That won't work," the other one replied. "He could still write everything down."

Not with my writer's block, Lyon thought to himself.

"We could go back to the island and get the ax for a job on his fingers," the smaller one suggested.

"I heard about a guy who learned to write with his toes."

"Yeah, I once saw a broad on TV who could type with this thing attached to her head. You see, Wentworth? It gets complicated."

"It's like everything in life," the man at the stern said.

"Once you start compromising, there's no place to stop. He's got to go over the side."

"Brumby and Stockton," Lyon said. "You two came out to my house with the hearse carrying the coffin."

"Take a lesson from this," Brumby said philosophically. "No matter how careful you are, you never can tell about people. Always kill all witnesses."

"I can see that you're right. I better shoot him in the head a couple of times first."

"Christ!" Brumby said. "You've got a lot to learn. In the first place shot sounds really carry over water, and second, you got to learn not to be so compulsive about things. Dead is dead and this is as good a spot as any to dump him."

The boat rocked precariously as the men changed position in order to lift Lyon up and begin to lever him over the side. "Wait!" Lyon yelled.

"We can't fool with you all night, you know," Brumby said as he dumped Lyon headfirst into the water.

He sank into the Sound for a few moments and felt a movement by his side as a heavy object passed. His body reversed itself with a jerk as the weight of the blocks tied to his feet turned him upright. He continued sinking toward the bottom.

"Anybody home?" Bea yelled from the vestibule as she tossed her purse on the silver tray on the hall table. She walked through the silent house. "Lyon! Pan?" She had often felt that Nutmeg Hill was peopled with ghosts, and that lusty bearded schooner captains still stalked the rooms. The emanations seemed strong tonight, and filled with foreboding. She hurried to a bank of light switches behind the drapes in the living room and threw several in haphazard fashion to light her home.

The patio lights were one of those that flicked on, along

with a flood that illuminated the rear yard. The barn door was open and their klunker station wagon was gone along with Pan's convertible. She wondered how he had managed to start the vehicle since she had both sets of keys in her purse.

In the kitchen she checked the refrigerator for the usual note he attached there when he went off on some errand. The small balloon-shaped magnet was there, but no note. In their bedroom she changed into comfortable shorts and kicked her shoes into a corner. The guest-room door was tightly closed.

Invading another person's private space had always been anathema to her, and even though it was *her* guest room, it was occupied by Pan at her invitation. She wasn't quite sure which shocked her more: her own act of turning the room's door handle, or the fact that she found the door locked.

They had carefully restored all the large brass locks on the bedroom doors, and each had a key resting in the lock. The keys were large, cumbersome affairs, hardly the kind that one would casually turn and drop in a pocket. She went downstairs to the pegboard in the kitchen and took down the master skeleton key. She hurried back up-stairs to unlock the sealed room.

It was a shambles. She backstepped in fear that intruders had ransacked the room. Then she realized that the mess was due to an almost studied slovenliness. The mattress on the bed was partially turned, the bedding bunched near the footboard. Clothing was strewn in small piles throughout the room, drawers were partly open, and damp towels were haphazardly draped over furniture. Bea began her search in the bureau, with the knowledge that she needn't take care in replacing items as she found them.

She found the large manila hasp envelope between the

mattress and box springs. She undid the clasp to find five tightly bundled packages of currency in one-hundred-dollar denominations. There was a ten-thousand-dollar mark band encircling each package of bills. She was staring down at fifty thousand dollars in cash.

"Collecting the room rent, honey?" Pan said from the doorway.

The cement blocks struck the bottom first. Lyon's bound feet brushed lightly against their top surface and then floated upward the length of the short line. He wondered how deep he was as it hadn't taken long to reach bottom. He was possibly in water less than thirty feet deep, but it was a moot point, since water only a few inches over his height would be sufficient to drown him.

He strained to separate his wrists, but the knots had been professionally tied. He was able to brush them along the rim of the game pouch in the rear of the vest he still wore. Their body search hadn't included the pouch, and he could still feel several objects near the small of his back. He was able to feel the outline of the candy bar and flat camera . . . and then, finally, the small bulk of the Swiss Army knife.

He worked his hands through the vent of the pocket and grasped the knife. He fumbled to open a blade, hoping that he'd lucked out and opened a cutting edge rather than corkscrew or magnifying lens.

The knife was open and he could feel a sharp edge. He tried to raise his feet, which resulted in his body jackknifing until he was able to reach the rope binding his feet. He began to saw at the rope as the pressure to gasp for breath increased. He hadn't had time to hyperventilate when they threw him overboard, and his only air was the last gasp he took before he went underwater.

The rope was cut. The knife slipped from his numb fingers as he scissored his legs to aid in the ascent. His slow rise seemed interminable, and he desperately wanted to gasp for air. A slow exhale relieved some of the pressure, but he knew it also reduced the length of time he could remain underwater without involuntarily gasping. His upward movement was impeded by the drag of wet clothing and the awkward rear position of his arms. He bicycled his legs faster and tilted his face upward in an involuntary effort to reach for the life-giving air that he needed.

He was going to drown. He had been unconscious for most of the final boat trip and had no knowledge of how far they had come. His sense of time was skewered, and he must have sunk far deeper than he'd suspected. He could be in the ocean, dumped in a depth that well exceeded the thirty feet he had estimated. He was drowning, and with that knowledge a lassitude began to seep through him.

His body broke the surface. The frantic whirl of his leg movements shot him waist-high out of the water before he fell back. He churned his legs again until the treading motion temporarily stabilized him on the surface and allowed him to gasp cool, spray-laden air.

Waves lapped at his head. A brisk breeze across the long ocean reach roiled the waters in a manner that could be fatal for him. His legs, fatigued from their frantic beat to the surface, were tiring. In a swimsuit, immersed in a warm pool or lake, and with free hands, he could stay afloat for hours. That wouldn't be possible under these conditions. The water was cool and he could cramp. The vest, which had saved his life a short time ago, was providing a heavy drag that might still drown him.

The moon was quartered and partially obscured by scudding clouds. As he rode on the crest of a swell he searched the blank horizon. No landmarks or shoreline was visible in any direction, nor could he see the running lights of any sailing vessels.

His hands fumbled for the flat life belt around his waist. It was still secure, but the inflation cartridge with its activator ring were at his right front and out of reach. He tried to force his hands toward the ring, but his movements only succeeded in dunking his head underwater.

The belt might turn. His fingers reached under the vest and felt for the belt. He touched its top edge and tugged. It moved. Only a slight, shift on his waist, but it had moved. He tugged again.

He gradually worked the belt around his body until he was able to slip a finger through the inflation ring. He pulled, and felt the pressure against his abdomen increase as the belt inflated. He would be able to slow his frantic leg scissoring and let the belt keep him afloat.

His head dipped underwater. Without the stabilizing effect of arm motion, the life belt at his waist was unstable. He would be able to keep afloat, but not in an upright position, and he would have to tread water carefully and breathe between waves.

He grimaced at the irony of his situation. He was half-saved, but several combinations of events could quickly drown him. There was also no way for him to make any forward motion, even if he knew the direction of the nearest landfall.

It was a question of time until he drowned.

On the one hand, Bea was acutely embarrassed for violating the basic rules of personal privacy; from another viewpoint, she was disturbed over her discovery of the large amount of hidden cash. "What's going on, Pan?"

The other woman strode across the room. Her hand lashed out and struck Bea across the face. The blow staggered Bea back against the wall and nearly caused her to lose her balance. "Stay out of my things, bitch!"

"I want you out of my house in half an hour," Bea said.

"What gave you the right to search my room? Do you

want to know what birth control I use? Or is it the designs of my panties that get you off?"

"I think you owe me an explanation about where that money came from," Bea said.

"I owe you nothing. Get out of my room. Move it, now!"

The audacity of the command dumbfounded Bea. She had spent over a hundred hours of hard work refinishing this room. Her sweat permeated the pores of the wood, and she could easily recall the ache of her knees after hours of scraping the floor molding. She picked up the packages of money and threw them.

One wrapping band burst in midair and showered bills over Pan. The other packages thudded against the far wall. Pan gave a small whimper and fell to her knees in order to gather the money strewn across the floor.

"I want you out of Nutmeg Hill as soon as you can possibly leave," Bea said with a quaver in her voice as she fought not to scream insults at the other woman.

"I have no place to go," Pan said in a childlike voice. "Please don't make me leave until Dalton gets back."

Bea stared in amazement at the woman before her on her knees frantically gathering up money. It was as if Pan had metamorphosed from the screaming shrew of moments before into a contrite child. "Where did the money come from, Pan?" Bea pressed in a level voice.

"Dalton gave it to me the morning of the day he disappeared. I was supposed to put it on the houseboat with the rest. I never got around to it."

"You knew there was more money hidden on the boat?"

"Dalton said he was getting it together to pay off the man who called at night."

"Do you know where Lyon went today?"

"No. I helped him start the car and he drove off in that old station wagon pulling a boat."

Bea glanced out the window into the dark night and then down at her wristwatch. It was far too late to be cruising on the Sound or river in a small runabout. She knew his thought patterns and musings often allowed him to solve intricate puzzles, and that might mean trouble. She ran for the phone.

"All right, I've got it," Rocco said over the telephone when she finally reached him at home. "It concerns me too. Give me the marker number of that old wagon of yours and I'll call the appropriate jurisdictions."

"BY three-forty-two," Bea said and after he repeated the plate number hung up. She walked numbly through the house and stopped in front of the bar cart where she began mixing a strong martini. She abruptly stopped. She would need every particle of concentration during the coming hours and liquor wouldn't help.

She wandered through the house until she came to the recreation room. She stood before the Ping-Pong table and looked down at the aerial map he had prepared. She had complained about the money for the map, the time he'd spent on the case; and this morning she had taken the car keys as if punishing a small child. Old-fashioned New England guilt made her shiver.

He had circled Red Deer Island on the map. She instantly knew that the small island was his destination. She rushed for the phone to call Rocco again. "He's gone out to an island," she blurted without preamble. "Can you arrange for a rescue boat to take us out there?"

"Boats are in short supply right now," Rocco said. "Word just came over my scanner that there's been an explosion followed by a fire on Red Deer Island. They're sending everything they've got out there to try and control it."

Lieutenant Commander Gregory Allcott, Coast Guard Academy '74, was very unhappy. Not only was this unexpected helicopter flight rumbling his new dress whites, but having to leave the dinner for the new Academy commandant in mid-course was not politically expedient. He tried not to glare at the diminutive woman huddled in a pea jacket by the open door, or her very large companion who was also staring out into the darkness. His eyes caught those of one of the airmen wearing a wetsuit. The diver shook his head and rolled his eyes at Bea.

Allcott knew the sailor's frustration. This was a patently ridiculous mission, instigated only because of political pressure. He tried talking to the woman, but his words were lost in the noise of the rotors. He motioned to her and then to the helmet by her side, which contained earphones and a microphone. She nodded and slipped the helmet on as he jacked in his own set.

"We can't see a damn thing down there, Senator Wentworth. We can fly much more effective search patterns at dawn."

"Keep flying."

Allcott realized that it wasn't a request. It was a command. Who the hell did this broad think she was? "You know, Senator, it wasn't necessary to call Senator Dodd to call the commander of the Coast Guard who called me. We always provide an adequate search for mariners in distress. At this time of night, this flight just isn't doing any good. We couldn't spot him if we were right over him."

Bea ignored his reasoning. "If you would please continue searching your side, Commander." She managed a small smile that quickly faded.

Allcott raised his night binoculars and swept the blackness below. What the hell, he thought. The guy probably burned to death on the island anyway.

Lyon heard the beat of the helicopter off to his right and turned his body in that direction. He instantly knew that without a flare, signal light of some sort, or radio signal, that they would never see or find him in time.

The only piece of equipment he had left was a waterlogged camera in the rear pouch. It had been immersed in the water from the moment he had been dumped overboard. It was all he had, and he fumbled clumsily in the rear pouch until he was able to extract the flat device. He awkwardly turned the unlocking lever and raised the flash unit. In order to fire it toward the sky, he would have to double over with his hands holding the camera raised behind his back while his head and upper body were submerged.

He ducked forward into the water while simultaneously jerking his bound hands to hold the camera upward. He pressed the shutter release and then raised his head to gulp air.

There was no way for him to determine if the flash was operative, but he would try again and again until the helicopter was out of sight and sound.

He ducked again and once more tripped the flash. It might work—after all, the camera was of Japanese manufacture.

"What's that?" Rocco said. "I think I saw something."

Bea was immediately at his side with her hand on his shoulder. "Where?"

"Off to the right." He pointed. "Something flashed. There it is again."

"I see it!" Bea said with excitement.

"Turn the searchlight to the right at nine o'clock!" Rocco yelled.

The searchlight beam danced across white caps below as it swiveled sides below the craft. "What do you have?" the Coast Guard officer asked over the engine sounds.

The flash blinked again. "A few feet to the stern!" Rocco thundered. The light hovered over the spot. "That's it!

"He's facedown in the water," Allcott said.

"Goddamn!" Rocco said as he stepped out the door of the helicopter.

10   Although he had learned to swim so young that he could hardly remember, Lyon's respect for the water verged on the pathological. He had an inordinate fear of drowning, and any choking sensation truly startled him. The warm lassitude he now felt was not fearful. He had once read that dying was not stressful, that the body released narcotic hormones that eased the passage. He felt himself drifting down a long, warm stream toward a distant light.

They had killed him! Two men, acting without remorse or thought, had nonchalantly tumbled him over the side of a boat. He would not make it easy for them. Somehow, somewhere, sometime, he would find them. He exerted every ounce of his remaining will to move.

"He's coming around," a faraway voice said.

Something warm and moist brushed his cheek. He opened his eyes to find Bea's face inches from his. "Oh, Lyon," she said.

"His vitals are steady," a nearby feminine voice said.

"I think I've been rescued," Lyon said. Bea kissed him on the forehead and rapidly turned away. He saw small tremors convulse her shoulders. The other bed in the room contained Rocco Herbert. "What's he doing here?"

"Sleeping on duty. What the hell do you think?" Rocco replied gruffly.

"Tweedledum and Tweedledee," Bea said. "You two ought to be incarcerated for your own protection."

Lieutenant Commander Allcott pushed past the doctor. "Are they going to live?" The doctor nodded. "Then I can call the commandant in Washington and tell him that we've got two for the price of one." He glared at Rocco. "You know, Chief, we had two experienced divers standing next to you. They were suited up and trained to make that jump. You almost botched our pickup to the point where we could have lost both of you."

"How in the hell was I to know that the water would be that cold?" Rocco said.

"Had you been drinking, Chief Herbert?"

"He's been seeing snakes recently," Lyon said.

Allcott shook his head. "I got a call to make," he said as he left.

"I found Dalton and the houseboat," Lyon said.

"Captain Norbert's been waiting in the hallway," Bea said. "Let me get him."

Captain Norbert, in full uniform and flanked by two State Police corporals, took up all the space along one wall of the narrow hospital room. "I told you to disappear, Wentworth. I warned you that we needed for you to disappear in society. So now you start lighting fires."

116

"Knock it off, Norbert," Rocco warned.

"If you weren't a victim of something I'd be working on charges now."

"What fire?" Lyon asked.

"There was an explosion and fire out on Red Deer Island."

Lyon sat up in bed. "Did you find Dalton's body?"

"We found what was left of somebody hanging on the wall of what was the master stateroom. Some perverted perp had done a knife job on him, but the ME thinks the hanging is what killed him. We're still sifting through the wreckage, but we'll have a positive ID soon."

"Okay, Lyon, tell us what happened out there," Rocco said.

Lyon took a moment to orient his still slightly confused thoughts. He attempted to put them in a logical order that would include everything of importance. He started by telling them about his initial suspicions concerning the island, and recounted all the subsequent events.

"Who were those slime?" Rocco asked when he was finished.

"They called themselves Brumby and Stockton when they came out to our house that day. I suspect that Dalton hired them for that particular prank and kept them on to help convert the houseboat. They were either told or discovered that there was a great deal of cash hidden on the boat, and then tortured Dalton to find out where he had hidden it."

"And then did a number on you when you walked in on them, and finally set the fire to cover their tracks," Rocco said.

"We bust those guys and we get the money and the killers," Norbert said.

"But who killed Katrina?" Bea asked.

"That case is closed," Norbert said. "I've got an airtight against Douglas. He's dead meat."

"As you can tell, Norbie likes to keep an open and objective mind about the suspects and evidence in a case," Rocco said to Lyon and Bea.

"If you weren't in a hospital bed, I'd beat your dumb brains out," Norbert growled.

Rocco swung his feet to the floor and pushed off the bed. "I'm not in bed anymore, liver lips."

Norbert held his hand, palm open, to the side, and a flanking State Police corporal immediately slapped the handle of a billy club into the captain's grasp. Bea immediately stepped between the two men. "I am a lady, and Rocco is not properly dressed for mortal combat."

Rocco looked down at the short johny gown that was obviously not designed for a man of his height and girth. He plopped back in bed and pulled a sheet up to his neck.

"Anything else happen of note while I was being murdered?" Lyon asked.

"Our houseguest has gone into emotional orbit and keeps fifty thousand dollars under her mattress," Bea said.

"That's a little heavy for a bread and butter gift," Lyon said.

"How about it was Dalton's money, which she forgot to put with the rest hidden on the houseboat, and maybe she was holding out on her partners, Messers. Brumby and Stockton."

"That's an interesting possibility," Rocco said.

Norbert growled. "You people don't do police work, you hold seances. I got to go." He tramped from the room followed by his uniformed entourage.

Bea looked thoughtful. "The only problem with Pan as a suspect is that she says she knew where the money was hidden. Why would Brumby and Stockton torture Dalton and take the houseboat apart if they were in it with Pan?"

"To make it look good," Rocco suggested.

"There's still Dice and Sam Idelweise," Lyon said as he swung his feet to the floor. "Let's go visit that island."

A towheaded resident stuck his head in the door. "I think you should leave now, Mrs. Wentworth. These men need rest."

Bea sighed. "Thank you, Doctor, but I think they have decided to go island hopping."

"They can't leave," the doctor said. "They have possible hypothermia, lung congestion, and they're both covered in bruises."

"The state cops did it to us," Rocco said as he pulled on damp pants.

The resident sank back against the wall. "The State Police beat the shit out of you and then dumped you in the Sound?"

"Those guys play hardball," Rocco said. "Watch yourself on I-ninety-five."

What remained of Red Deer Island looked like a small Pacific atoll that the Marines and Japs had fought over during World War II. Little foliage remained on what few trees were left, and the houseboat had been reduced to a skeleton of charred timbers that held no resemblance to the past grandeur of the craft.

The young police officer piloting the Boston Whaler ran it up on the small beach as far as he could. Rocco and Lyon gingerly stepped over the gunnels and limped in unison toward the remains of the *Mississippi.* "How did a fire do all that?" Lyon asked.

"It was a hell of a lot more than a fire," Rocco replied. "There were a couple of explosions that were too powerful to be accounted for by propane or fuel tanks going up. The fire marshal's office thinks there was plastique involved."

"Oh, that's interesting." Lyon stepped gingerly through the rubble. He looked down at the ground as if searching.

"Norbie's men and the lab guys have been going over the ground with sieves."

"Why?" Lyon asked.

"You know that lab work is extensive in any crime like this."

"I don't mean that. I mean why did they go to the trouble of blowing the thing up?"

"These guys aren't exactly brain surgeons, you know. They spent a couple of days tearing the boat apart, and knew they'd left prints and god only knows what else all over the place. Ten to one they have priors, so they took the lazy way out and torched the whole damn floating castle."

"You two get over here," Norbert said with a beckoning gesture.

They stepped gingerly through the wreckage as they made their way to where officers were carefully sifting through debris that had been part of the master stateroom. "Whatcha got?" Rocco asked.

"Show them."

They stood in a small circle around a kneeling technician. A plastic sheet had been spread over the mutilated decking, and centered on it was a small metal box approximately eight inches by four. It had evidently been wrapped in heavy paper that, although charred, had been carefully removed and placed to the side.

"There's writing on the paper," the technician said. "I can't make it out, but we'll be able to raise it in the lab. I'd guess from the configurations that it's an address."

"Cut the lectures and find out what's in the box," Norbert demanded.

"We might get latents from the exterior," the tech said in pique.

"We might get a letter of reprimand in our personnel file if we don't do what the captain orders," Norbert said.

"I'm doing it, okay?" He bent over the small box with a pair of tweezers and gently raised the lid. "Beautiful, just beautiful," he said.

Lyon bent over the tech's shoulder and peered into the box. Resting on a bed of cotton gauze was an unburned human finger. It wore a wide gold wedding band. "Can you get prints from it?"

"Can I get prints? Wow, can I get prints," the tech said as he slipped the box and finger into an acetate evidence bag. "This baby is perfect."

"Dalton was an army officer, so we know his prints will be on file," Lyon said.

Rocco and Lyon walked to the end of the island and sat on a fallen log. A brisk wind ruffled their hair, and white-caps danced in the distance. The island was still a barren place, as if its soul had been wrenched away. Confused birds circled overhead and occasionally alighted on charred branches.

"Just before those guys dumped me overboard they made a joking reference to taking a walk on Narragansett Bay," Lyon said.

Rocco looked at him sharply. "That's interesting. Seems that I remember your friend in Cranston, Rhode Island, as having a past interest in that type of aquatic sport."

Captain Norbert walked past the log where they sat and stood with his feet at the edge of the water. He looked out over the Sound toward the distant tip of Long Island. "This place wouldn't make a bad spot for a summer place. I'd bulldoze off the crap that's left and throw up an A-frame. 'Course, you'd need a satellite dish for the old TV."

"It's a bird sanctuary, Norbie," Rocco said.

"So, let the birds stay as long as they don't do-do over

the barbecue. This place will be all right once we find all the body parts."

"Where was Katrina killed?" Lyon asked.

Norbert shrugged as if to dispel his dreams of summer grandeur and his mental flagstoning of the island. "You mean the Loops decedent? The ME says odds are she was knocked off where we found her and not more than a couple of hours before. It fits our time frame for Douglas."

"Was she prone when she was stabbed?" Lyon asked.

"What difference does it make?"

"The force required and the angle of penetration would differ according to her position," Lyon said.

"The Medical Examiner said that the blade went in at a straight angle. The killer was either straddling her or kneeling next to her. The perp may or may not have used two hands to make the thrust."

"It would only take one hand if the guy had power," Rocco said.

"You ever see the arms on Douglas?" Norbert said.

"I found another piece," a searching trooper yelled.

"It's mine, mine, mine," MacIntire yelled out.

"Your men are sick, Norbie," Lyon said.

"If you had to search for body parts for two days you'd indulge in a little black humor too," Rocco said in the men's defense.

Bea had the household bills separated into neat piles on the breakfast-room table. She chewed on the tip of a ballpoint pen as she contemplated the open checkbook.

Lyon poured them each coffee as he thought about the force necessary to drive a slim-bladed knife through a person's sternum.

"Do you know what it costs to heat this barn?" Bea asked.

"I would have thought there would have been bruises on her chest," Lyon mused.

"We are not on the same wave length, in fact, we aren't even in the same solar system. You inhabit a parallel universe, Wentworth. Do you know that?"

"An ordinary person would have made the thrust more to the right, rather than directly into the myocardial sac," Lyon said.

"That proves it." Bea snicked the phone from its wall bracket before the second ring. "Hello . . . Yes, Governor, Senator Dodd was very cooperative . . . the Commandant of the Coast Guard also. . . . They were not using a Coast Guard helicopter as a swimming platform. They were not drunk and I will not remove my day-care amendment from the bill." She hung up.

"It almost makes you believe in anarchism," Lyon said as the phone rang again. "I'll handle him. Hello." He listened intently for a few moments and then slowly hung up.

"You really told him off, Went."

"It was Rocco. The prints on the finger were Dalton's. They have traced the ring on the severed finger to Dalton. The lab reconstructed the writing on the paper wrapping on the finger box and found that it was to Pan's address at the resort. Dalton is dead. What I saw has been verified."

Bea closed the checkbook. "Those bastards were going to send Dalton's severed finger with his wedding band to Pan?"

"Evidently. He was obviously their prisoner from the beginning. When they had the money and found out from him that Pan had the missing fifty thousand, they probably intended to extort it from her until I interrupted things."

The front door slammed. "Is that you, Pan?" Bea called.

She was answered by feet running up the stairs and the resounding slam of the guest-room door. The thick walls of the old house were insufficient to muffle the sound of crashing drawers and slamming doors.

"She's broken up over Dalton," Lyon said. "Why don't you go to her?"

"We aren't on the best of terms since my shakedown of her room. You had better offer the tea and sympathy."

The clatter in the guest room continued as Lyon mounted the stairs and knocked on the door. He knocked a second time without response and finally called out, "Pan, it's Lyon."

The door snapped open. Her tense face was framed angrily in the opening. "What the hell do you want? Make it snappy. I got to blow this place."

"We're both sorry about Dalton. Is there anything we can do?"

"Are you kidding? Cut the crap! There's going to be dancing in the streets when the world learns that Dalton the prankster has really gone to that great joke-land-in-the-sky. He didn't have many friends, or did I say that before?"

"I owed him something, and I'll never forget that."

"Well, you found him, and that makes it even. I gave him a shot at marriage and he blew it. So, I'm even. He left me a third of the partnership insurance, and now I'm in bed with those two dingbats, Sam and Randy. I'm going to help them finish the resort job, and then I'm taking my third of the profits and blowing the country."

"You're a partner?"

"I always was on paper. Dalton said it was for tax reasons."

"Why did he leave?"

She continued picking up heaps of clothing from the floor and stuffing them haphazardly into a suitcase. "The disappearing boat trick came in handy when the IRS got too close, and the man who phoned in the night started getting serious."

"And you end up with fifty thousand in mad money and a third of the business?" Lyon said.

She tried to close the suitcase, but protruding items kept the locking clasps inches apart. She plunked down on it with her full weight and forced it closed. "Your sneaky wife has a big mouth."

"We've tried to help you through a difficult period in your life."

"I'm finished with my difficult period and now I'm going." She hefted the bag and struggled toward the door.

"Let me help you with that," Lyon said.

"Thanks, but no thanks." She pulled the suitcase along the carpet and thumped it down the stairs.

Bea stood at the foot of the stairs and looked up with concern. "Are you all right, Pan?"

The suitcase slid off the last step and Pan dragged it toward the front door, but paused to look at them. "I'm just glad to get away from you nosy people."

"What's going on with her?" Bea asked. "I apologized for going through her things."

"Methinks she doth protest too much," Lyon said as he brushed past Pan to stand before the front door and face her with a slightly bemused smile. "I have a few questions that concern Katrina, money, and the fact that you were the only person in the world who knew I was going out in the boat that day."

"I'm not going to answer any of your dumb questions," Pan said. "You people must get your kicks this way."

"If you prefer, I'll let Rocco do the asking."

Pan faced Bea in a manner that excluded Lyon. "I knew he'd try something when I tried to leave. He's been hitting on me since the night I arrived at this dump."

"I don't believe that, Pan," Bea said levelly.

"I finally let him. I just got tired of all the hassle, you know. I guess I also felt I owed him something, and so I let him do it a couple of times. Now he's pissed because I told him it's over."

"I don't believe that either, Pan," Bea said quietly.

"Oh, you don't? You probably think that you're the greatest lay in the world. Well, Miss Great Screw, he begged for someone younger who wasn't over the hill."

Bea laughed. "Oh, honey child. I've been gone after by real experts. You can't reach me that way."

"You still don't believe that I made it with your husband?"

"No, I don't. I'd stake my life on it."

Pan bent closer to Bea as if to whisper conspiratorially, but the words were more than loud enough. "I can prove it. He's the only man I ever had, and I've had a lot, who yells 'eureka' when he makes it."

A stunned Bea took two involuntary steps backward. Her mouth gaped open.

"Gotcha," Pan said as she dragged her bag through the door and across the drive to her car.

11 They stood at opposite ends of the large country kitchen as the car careened down the drive, noisily spewing gravel. Tears brimmed in her eyes. Her hands hung loosely at her sides, and she tilted slightly forward, her head lowered against her chest.

"I know I'm being dumb," she said in a voice he could barely hear. "This sort of thing sometimes happens when you've been married a long time. I know it's not the end of the world, but why does it hurt so much?"

"It didn't happen." He stepped toward her, but she scurried out of his way and kept the center chopping block between them. She folded her arms across her breasts as if to ward off his touch.

"Don't ever try to con a politician, Wentworth," she said. "We're experts in that area." Her voice had changed to a sharp cutting tone.

"I swear to you . . ."

"It's all over and she's gone. Just do me the favor of not seeing her again."

"It's the word of an agitated young woman against mine."

"It's not a question of her word, Went. It's *your* word that she repeated. I have never heard or read of anyone else in the world who said 'eureka' when they made love."

"I'm not that unique. Lots of people must say it."

"If they did, the word would become generic. People would go around saying, gee, that was such a great play, book, steak, or what have you, that I nearly eureka-ed. It would become scatological, kids would write the 'E' word in inappropriate places. You are unique and unusual, Lyon, and only you say 'eureka.'"

"Pan didn't want to answer my questions and went on the offensive."

"Where do you get the energy?" She left the room and walked out the French doors onto the patio as Lyon answered the phone.

She didn't turn to face him, but continued looking out over the river as he joined her on the patio. "That was Randy Dice on the phone. He's holding some sort of memorial service for Dalton at his house tonight."

"You can't stay away from her, can you?"

"Pan won't be there."

"What time is the service?"

"Nine."

"That's a little late, isn't it?" She turned to face him. The tears were gone and her eyes narrowed as she looked at him. "But it does give us time for you to tell me about the others."

*　　*　　*

Lyon drove down the drive after an uncomfortable hour-and-a-half. Bea had followed him through the house insisting that he confess to all his past infidelities. He had finally capitulated and admitted his affairs.

"There have only been three," he had said, "Elizabeth Taylor, Queen Elizabeth the Second, and Brooke Shields."

"That's ridiculous!" Bea had snorted. "You're too old for Brooke Shields."

He glanced at the dashboard clock. It was still two hours until the start of the memorial service. Since the atmosphere at Nutmeg Hill was less than hospitable, he had decided to use the time to speak with Sam Idelweise.

Sam lived in Wessex, a town midway between Murphysville and the resort project. The house was a brick ranch with a lawn bordered with flower beds that Bea would have appreciated. As Lyon parked in the drive, his first impression was that a lawn maintenance crew was busy at work. A second glance sorted out Sam edging a walk, a broad-hipped woman in jeans planting fledgling tomato plants with her daughter, and an adolescent boy cutting broad sweeps of grass on a sit-down mower.

Sam waved at Lyon. "Come meet the family before I pop us a beer."

After introductions they talked moles and crabgrass for a few minutes. Evidently the family considered both events as nothing less than catastrophic. Lyon had always thought that moles were rather benign creatures who made interesting burrows. The Idelweise family considered the rodents as nothing less than a scourge of mankind who should be obliterated on discovery.

"Mole alert!" a cracking adolescent voice called from the mower. The complete family was immediately galvanized into action that was obviously part of a well-planned and practiced tactical assault. The mower boy produced a pitchfork and proceeded to jab it violently into the newfound burrow. Mother and daughter ran for the house and returned with a large canister whose hose nozzle proceeded to spray a noxious foam into the pitchfork apertures. Sam appeared from the rear porch with a .410 shotgun. He proceeded to stalk the ground as diligently as any combat soldier.

The shotgun boomed. "Got the sucker," Sam said as he held the tattered remains of a small rodent aloft by the tail. He deposited his trophy in a rear garbage can and called to Lyon, "Let's have that beer."

Lyon wondered if protecting the home from devious rodents fell into the same category as removing Dalton-like threats. He followed Sam into the kitchen whose glossy floor reflected their images.

Sam popped two ice-cold cans of Bud and handed one to Lyon. He sipped contentedly on his beer as he leaned against the refrigerator. "You see why I was so upset with Dalton." He waved his hand expansively toward the remainder of the house. "I would have lost all of this. My family would have ended up living in some goddamn house trailer. I'd be carrying boards for some two-bit contractor."

"You don't seem at all worried now. Has the partnership insurance kicked in?"

"We talked to the broker this afternoon. Thanks to you, they accepted identification of Dalton's body and cleared us for payment. Which means it's going to save the goddamn job, my house, and everything else that I own."

"I understand that Pan is a part owner of the corporation," Lyon said.

A slight scowl washed across Sam's face. "Well, you got to take the good with the bad. She's a fucking space cadet."

"How do you and Randy Dice get along?"

"He's the uptight asshole financial guys usually are, but

I think we each got our territory staked out. If he sticks to running the money end and leaves me alone with the construction, we'll make a good team. You know, Wentworth, I think it just might work. We're going to pull the job through and maybe even make a few bucks. And we're free from that crazy bastard Dalton."

"As a matter of curiosity, where were you the night Dalton disappeared, and also the night of the fire on the island?"

"You mean the night you almost bought it?"

"That's right."

"I was downstairs in my workshop."

"Both times?" Lyon asked.

"Recently, I've been down there every night. When I get upset I work with wood, and with Dalton's goings-on I was climbing the walls so bad I had to work down there. It's more effective than booze. Come on, I'll show you."

Without waiting for Lyon's answer, Sam opened the cellar door and threw the light switch before disappearing down the stairs. Lyon followed.

The wood smell was apparent halfway down the steps. It was a good odor of aged wood, sawdust, and the faint residue of machine oil. The cellar was crowded with machinery: several types of power saws, a wood lathe, and two workbenches with a myriad of tools attached neatly above them. It was an orderly and functional place administered by a man who obviously loved tools and the materials they shaped.

Sam stopped by a small pile of wood on a bench and picked up a single two-foot section. He ran his fingers gingerly along its grain. "Look at this piece. It's what I'm going to work with next." He held it toward Lyon. "Isn't it great?"

The wood was extremely fragrant. "What is it?" Lyon asked.

"Sandalwood. I've never worked with it before, but it's been used in Asian cabinetwork for generations. I'm really looking forward to shaping it."

Lyon rubbed his fingers along the smooth grain of the wood. "By the way, did you see Katrina the morning she was killed?"

Sam picked up a hammer from the workbench and slammed it onto a hook in a pegboard. "If I had, I would have said so! You know, Wentworth, I gave the cops all that information." He glared at Lyon a moment and then some of the anger seemed to dissipate. "No, I did not see Katrina that day. I was making all those damn phone calls to the marinas trying to locate the houseboat. I never went to the cottages or near the water that morning."

"Then you and Dice were both in the office that morning?"

"Yes, except that Randy was gone part of the time. He said he had a meeting with some money guy he knew and was going to try and negotiate something."

"Then you were alone part of the time and Randy was gone part of the time?" Lyon said.

"So? Jesus! Why in the hell would I want to knock off Kat Loops? And what difference do these questions make anyhow? I understand they got quite a case against Bobby Douglas."

"Maybe," Lyon said. "I'm still convinced that the two men on the houseboat weren't in on it alone. Someone had to tip them off to the fact that there was a great deal of money on the boat."

"It's over, Wentworth. Let it drop." He went to the far end of the room and stopped before a smaller workbench where a dropcloth was spread over several objects. "I'd like you to see what I've been working on. Turn your back until I set them up."

Lyon turned, sure that he would be able to make the

appropriate remarks concerning the craftsmanship of the display. All the other finished pieces that he could see were of excellent quality.

"Look at my beauties," Sam said.

Lyon looked down at the small display spread neatly over the bench. Sam had turned a light so that its beam fell squarely on the models. "My God."

"I decided to work in miniature," Sam said. "Some of the devices are just too large for storage, so I work on a one-to-ten scale in exact replica. But every single device is fully functional."

"I can believe it," Lyon said in amazement. The display consisted of intricate miniatures of every item in the most complete medieval torture chamber, along with scale models of death machines of several states and a few foreign countries. The fatal devices consisted of a guillotine, electric chair, and an exact duplicate of the San Quentin gas chamber, along with a full working model of a hangman's scaffold. The inquisitor's tools were the rack, iron maiden, and other devices that Lyon couldn't identify.

"Let me show you how they work," Sam said with pride. "My favorite is the guillotine." Before Lyon could reply he whisked a Barbie doll out from under the bench and forced the toy into a kneeling position with her head resting over the tiny wicker basket and her neck properly aligned for the execution. Drawn upward by a thin wire, the blade of the machine slowly rose.

Lyon's hand flicked forward as his fingers pinched the guillotine blade against its supports. "I get the idea. I know the thing works and don't need a full demonstration."

"Aren't these things great?" Sam asked with obvious pride.

"I'd say it's a very unusual collection."

"You want to hear the snap of the trap door when I hang one?"

"I'll take your word for it," Lyon said. "Sam, do you always use little blond dolls with long legs and hair to their shoulders?"

"Jesus, Wentworth! It's a question of economics. I can buy a fake Barbie for two bucks at a discount house. Those damn Ken dolls would run me ten or twelve bucks apiece. What's the matter with you? Do you think I'm some sort of pervert?"

During the short drive to the Dice home, Bea's conversation seemed to consist mostly of numbers. "Thirty." No answer. "All right, more than twenty but less than fifty?"

"The writer George Simenon in his autobiography claimed to have made love to a thousand women in his lifetime," Lyon said and immediately regretted the remark.

Bea blanched, and considered the possibility a moment. "In Simenon's case that's about one woman for each book he wrote. If you operate on that scale, and considering your recent productivity, we don't have a problem."

"Touché," Lyon said. Long marriages invariably gave each partner knowledge of the most painful buttons to push.

"We now seem reduced to an even baker's dozen," she said. "And I don't know why I'm going on like this except that it's like an aching tooth. It's there, it hurts, and still you can't help sloshing your tongue around to see how bad it can really get."

The Dices lived in a new Murphysville subdivision called Herkimer Heights. The location had once been the town dump. Years of use had finally filled the area to capacity. The town fathers had bulldozed a thin layer of topsoil over the refuse and sold the land to Leon Herkimer, a former used-car salesman. The houses listed for three hundred thousand, but Leon would deal, particularly if the prospective buyers noticed the abundance of sea gulls nostalgically circling the lots.

The Dice driveway and street frontage were filled with an eclectic assortment of vehicles. Brand-new Porsches and BMW's sat next to rusting Fords and dusty pickup trucks. The house's north wall had already cracked as the foundation made its inexorable tip to the side in the flimsy landfill.

A pleasantly warm dusk had settled comfortably over the area. There was light in every window of the Dice home, and guests overflowed onto the rear deck and swimming pool. As Lyon and Bea went up the walk toward the front door, they were deluged with party sounds.

"This is obviously not one of your more sedate memorial services," Bea said.

The front door was ajar, and they stepped inside to be met by Randy Dice. "Is that you, Dice?" Lyon asked quizzically. The man before them bore little resemblance to the overly worried financial officer at the resort. His usual conservative suit had been shucked and replaced by madras Bermuda shorts, a loud Hawaiian sport shirt, and beaded moccasins. Conversation was drowned by the living room's four-speaker stereo system, which began blaring the Doors' "Light My Fire."

Dice kept a strong grip on both their arms as he steered them through the crowd toward the bar. "You're my buddy, Wentworth. I mean, you really saved the day, drove the Huns from the streets, held the pass with a loyal band, saved our ass, in other words. He's dead and gone and we are back in business."

"Finding Dalton's body is hardly something I need be thanked for," Lyon said.

"The other half has arrived," Randy said and led them back to the front door. A woman of thirty, carrying a briefcase, stood in the doorway. She watched the swirling party through horn-rimmed glasses with an uncertain gaze. Her abundant jet-black hair was in a French twist, and her somber Givenchy business suit was of modest length. Dice introduced his wife, Maureen, and told them that she was a bond analyst in Hartford.

"Randy and I were at Harvard Business together," Maureen said.

Bea, standing slightly in back of Maureen, held up two fingers for Lyon to see. They both knew that a record had been established that might never be broken in their lifetime.

"The Dillworths are down from Portland, the MacKenzies from Boston, and a host of others, honeypot. Those people don't come to just any affair."

"I can see it's going to be a great party," Maureen said in a small voice.

"I guess Dalton would have appreciated a party as much as a memorial service," Lyon said.

"Memorial service!" Dice chortled. "This is a celebration that the rat is gone."

"Which, I take it, is why Pan Turman is not here," Bea asked.

"Neither Mr. or Mrs. Turman was welcome in my house after a certain incident at the resort," Maureen Dice said.

Randy Dice finished his drink and his already-flushed face turned a deeper hue of red. "We made the mistake of accepting an invitation to spend a night at the resort. The next morning at breakfast they made all sorts of sly remarks about convertible debentures, friendly takeovers, and leveraged buy-outs."

"I don't understand," Bea said.

Maureen blushed. "Well, convertible debentures are my . . . and friendly takeovers and buy-outs are when Randy and I . . . make love."

"They had a damn microphone planted in our mattress," Randy said. "A little joke they evidently pulled many times."

"Eureka," Bea said. "And so goes Elizabeth Taylor."

"She trifled with me," Lyon said.

"You have to get ready for the party," Dice told his wife as he led her away.

"I don't know a soul at this party," Bea said. "I can't understand it. I know most of the voters in my district at least by sight. Let's see if we can meet some of them."

Maureen Dice made her second appearance a few minutes later. She exited from the bedroom with a loud "Ta Dum!," which caused a small circle of admirers to gather appreciatively around her with Lyon and Bea on the periphery of the group. Maureen had changed radically. Her long raven hair now hung in an abundant shower down her back, and she wore a skimpy halter and very tight short-shorts. She held her hands up in the air and did a bump-and-grind routine.

Randy Dice stood directly behind them. "Now you see what I would have lost if the job went under. She would never stay with me if I went belly up."

"People often surprise you in their reaction to adversity," Bea said.

"Maureen knows as well as I that it's survival of the fittest. That's economic determinism pure and simple. Do the other guy before he does you. You only get screwed if you don't understand those rules," Dice said.

"It seems to me that your financial salvation was due more to a quirk of fate, rather than any Machiavellian moves on your part," Lyon said.

"We make our own opportunities," Dice replied.

"Where were you the night Dalton disappeared?" Lyon asked.

Dice squinted at him with what might have been a smile. "You saw me talk to him on the boat that afternoon, and it was obvious to everyone that I had to talk to one of our banks. It was a long dinner meeting, and I stayed over at a Hartford motel."

"Which one?"

"I don't remember. It might have been one in the suburbs, I don't recall."

"The name and location would be on your credit card receipt."

"I paid cash." He put one arm on Lyon's shoulder and another around Bea in a move that was both alcoholic camaraderie and an effective change of subject. "It never would have occurred to me to invite you two to one of our parties if Dalton hadn't told me that you really liked to swing. Enjoy." He moved off into the crowd.

"Dalton's still haunting us," Lyon said.

"They've begun skinny-dipping in the pool," Bea said. "I fear the witching hour approaches and we'll soon be asked to participate in the fun and games."

Lyon nodded, and they moved in unspoken unison toward the front door.

They were halfway down the drive when they heard the slap of bare feet on the grass behind them. They turned to see Maureen rushing toward them. She plucked at Bea's sleeve. "Please don't go. Everything's just starting."

"We're not prudes," Bea said. "But we're just not into swinging."

"You don't have to participate." There was a girlish imploring in her nearly desperate request.

"I'm afraid voyeurism isn't our bag either," Lyon said.

"I didn't mean that, I thought maybe we could just

talk." She turned to look back at the house where several lights had already been extinguished. "I don't know what I meant, except that I'm not into it either. Randy thinks that I am because I pretend. I come home, change my clothes, and put on an act with all the appropriate words and noises. When it comes time to do it, I hide in the linen closet. Everyone thinks that I select someone special, but I don't. I hide."

Bea took the other woman's hand. "Why do you pretend?"

"Because that's what he wants. I'm really so plain and dull, and he could have lots of other women. Thanks for coming, anyway." She began to walk slowly back to the house as another light went out.

12

Lyon sat lengthwise on their parapet above the Connecticut River with his knees drawn up to his chin. He faced toward the Sound as a mild breeze marched upriver carrying the smell of the night sea. There seemed to be a metallic taste in his mouth, and he felt a sheen of depression. The Dice party and the earlier tour of Sam's pain-evoking machines merged into differing groups of unpleasant pictures.

He tried to reconcile Sam's miniature torture chamber within the parameters of normal social behavior. Adult men often collected toy soldiers or built model warships. Was that worse than duplicating the Inquisition's implements? He answered his own question: there was a certain misplaced grandeur in ancient battles; but it was difficult to find any vestige of glory in the dank dungeons of medieval castles.

The daytime Randolph Dice often seemed a caricature. His swinging nights were an aberration that would eventually destroy his wife.

"I found it under the mattress," Bea said as she slipped the small transmitter into his hand. "What are you so pensive about?"

"I'm thinking rotten thoughts about people I talked to tonight."

She sat on the wall next to him and hugged her shoulders in the slight chill. She wore a short nightgown that barely covered her upper thighs. "Your trouble is that you are an incorrigible romantic and I'm freezing my bottom off out here."

"I don't think it's unreasonable to expect that people you know don't construct torture instruments or hold sex orgies."

"You have forgotten that someone we know has been doing very bad things to other people we knew. A man and woman are dead, and the man died in great pain."

"What connection do you make?" Lyon asked.

"I see one couple's very expensive lifestyle, another man who is fascinated with pain, and a widow who is off the wall. Then, all of a sudden we find that these three have a great deal to gain financially if Dalton is dead."

"Do you think they operated individually or in concert?" Lyon asked.

"I just can't see that group working together in some murderous cabal," Bea said. "But I can imagine any one of them using Brumby and Stockton. My buns are numb, Went."

He crossed the patio and snicked her sweater from the back of a chair in the living room. He draped it carefully over her shoulders. "I thought modern women got their own clothing."

"Not when they are utilizing their vast deductive powers to solve a crime so that their husbands can go back to work and make money to pay last winter's oil bill."

"We shouldn't forget my friend in Cranston, Rhode Island," Lyon said. "Before those two goons dumped me in the drink, they made a remark about taking a walk on Narragansett Bay. That's a body of water that Carillo staked out in the past, and I find the remark highly coincidental."

"We'll pass on that possibility for tonight," Bea said. She slipped off the wall and let the sweater fall as she stretched. Lyon noticed that the cool air had done some interesting things to her top half, and the stretching motion had hiked the gown over her hips to make her bottom half also quite interesting. "Coming to bed?" she said in a low voice.

"I'll be right up," he said as he watched her bend over to pick up the fallen sweater.

She smiled. "I think you have the right to more than equal Simenon, even if it is with the same person. Hurry."

He went into the kitchen and dialed Rocco. "I want us to go up to Rhode Island tomorrow," Lyon said without preamble.

"I'm game," Martha Herbert answered. "Are we going to the motel before we tour the Newport mansions?"

"That can only be Wentworth," Rocco's voice boomed over his wife's as he took the phone.

Lyon reddened. "Tell Martha that I'm sorry I was so abrupt."

"She says she lusts for you too. Now, what's this about Rhode Island?"

* * *

There was a desolate look to the narrow house with the pink flamingo in the front yard. Rocco punched the front door chime for the third time, and again they heard the first bars of "Ave Maria" echo through the interior. "Maybe our friend decided to take a hasty trip to Salerno."

Lyon took a turn at the door and pushed the chime again. He heard shuffling footsteps on the other side. A latch bolt clicked, and the door opened the few inches the night chain allowed. In the dim light beyond the narrow aperture he saw a slight figure in a long bathrobe wearing what seemed to be a terry-cloth towel wrapped around its head.

"Go away." He recognized the frightened voice.

"Take the chain off, Maria," Lyon ordered.

The door closed, the night chain clinked against the inside panel, and reopened as Maria, holding the towel over her face as if imitating a Moslem, retreated before them. "I have a bad case of poison ivy," she mumbled. "You better not get near me."

Lyon stepped to her and gently pulled the towel from her head.

"Good God!" Rocco said. "Someone beat the hell out of her."

Maria's face was swollen into a mottled, dark-blue mask. Her movements were studied, as if the slightest twitch caused tendrils of pain. Her hair, once combed into a neat sheen that fell down her back, was stringy and disheveled. Rocco went to her. His large hands gently touched her face as he viewed the damage with a professional eye. "Who did this to you, girl?"

She retreated until the banister stopped her motion. "I fell down the stairs."

"How many times?" Rocco asked.

"Your grandfather did this," Lyon said.

She turned her head toward the wall without answering.

"Where is he?" Rocco asked more harshly than he had intended.

She cringed from the large police officer and stumbled on the stairs. As she fell, she grasped the banister with both hands. "Please don't hit me," she said in a whimper.

Rocco knelt next to the young girl and put his arms around her. It was a natural gesture that Lyon had seen his friend make countless times before as he soothed the hurt of Remley, his own daughter. Maria seemed to inchoately sense this, and she buried her head in the chief's shoulder as small tremors racked her shoulders.

"Where is your Poobah now?" Lyon asked.

The tremors continued a few moments longer before she gave a muffled answer. "At the restaurant where he goes everyday."

"And where is that?" Lyon asked softly.

Antonio's was located in a seedy section of Providence that had once housed streets of Italian emigrants. The Portuguese had replaced the Italians and in turn had been supplanted by Puerto Ricans. The restaurant had retained its identity regardless of the neighborhood's change in ethnicity. Hardly a dozen tables with checked tablecloths with candles stuck in empty Chianti bottles occupied the narrow interior. An old brass cash register sat on a plain table near the rear double doors that led to the kitchen. The room was devoid of customers as they entered.

A small bell above the door tinkled as it opened, and shortly a white-haired waiter with rheumy eyes and three days' stubble pushed through the rear doors. "We ain't open yet."

"Get Carillo," Rocco said.

"Who wants him?"

"God! Now, move it," Rocco said.

The waiter's mouth moved silently a few times as if in preparation for a proper retort, but after another glance at Rocco he shrugged and went back into the kitchen. A heavier and younger face with flat eyes peered out the door's window port.

"I think the dwarf Grumpy is preparing to have words with us," Lyon said as they sat at a nearby table.

Grumpy erupted through the doors and lumbered toward them. He was dressed in a rumpled seersucker suit with a dress shirt that was spattered with tomato sauce. His narrow eyes were pushed into even smaller dimensions by the rise of fleshy cheekbones. In two strides he was at the table, and in a quick and abrupt movement whose speed was surprising for his size, had jerked Lyon up and over the table. Hamlike hands passed over Lyon's body in an efficient weapons search. He let Lyon sag back in the chair and started around the table toward Rocco.

Rocco raised his palm a few inches off the table. "Don't do it, friend."

Grumpy did not pause as his hands reached for Rocco's jacket collar. The police chief's chair pitched backward as in a single fluid movement he rose, stepped to the side, and jerked the man's hand forward and upward behind his back. Increasing the pressure on the arm to force Grumpy to hunch forward, Rocco spun him forward and careened him back through the kitchen door. Rocco returned to his seat at the satisfying sound of clattering pots and pans.

Angie Carillo had a frozen smile on his face as he pushed through the doors and walked over to the table. "Ah, Mr. Wentworth. You honor me with a return visit. Perhaps you have heard of Antonio's? He is preparing one of his magnificent specialties for today: pasta with shrimp and pears stuffed with gorgonzola cheese."

"Did you obtain two men called Brumby and Stockton for Dalton Turman?" Lyon asked without preamble.

"Men are not serfs, Mr. Wentworth. They work for those who pay. There are some who are employed by my enterprises for a time, move on, and then return as the need arises."

"He's being cute," Rocco said in a dead voice. "You want that I should redecorate this place?"

"We have help in the kitchen who would prevent that," Carillo said.

"You got more than five back there?" Rocco asked as he flipped open his jacket wide enough for the shoulder holster containing the .357 Magnum to be visible.

"Chief Herbert is often difficult to control," Lyon said as he picked up on his role. "I'll ask you once more about Brumby and Stockton."

Carillo's hands splayed out in an expressive shrug. "We had some slow times recently, and Mr. Turman needed some help with one of his famous pranks. I believe it had something to do with a hearse and coffin. I provided two men for that task and some other minor chores Mr. Turman had in mind."

"Such as helping him disappear?" Lyon said.

"It would seem as if that is how it turned out," Carillo said.

"They tried to kill me," Lyon said.

"They were obviously inefficient."

"We believe they killed Dalton for the money he had hidden on the houseboat. I should also point out that some of that money could have been yours."

Carillo's fingers fluttered. "Every business sustains losses?"

"We want to find those men," Lyon said.

"That should not be difficult since they are both gamblers. Such men have no choice when they carry money. They go to Vegas or Atlantic City. That is where they will be. Perhaps you will try the chicken with couscous? It is very good here."

"You don't seem very concerned over your loss?"

"Such matters are taken care of one way or the other," Carillo said.

"We're interested in what you mean by 'other,'" Rocco said.

Carillo stood up. "Since you are not tempted by our good food, there is nothing more to say."

"Your men killed Dalton, tried to kill Lyon, and all of a sudden you don't give a damn about money or the guys who did it," Rocco said. "I don't believe you, Carillo. You stink."

Carillo smiled. It was not an ordinary smile, but one that somehow managed to convey a great sense of menace and hostility. "You dishonor me, Chief Herbert. If we both did not understand the rules so clearly, you would not return home tonight."

"I saw what you did to your granddaughter," Rocco said in a voice that had dropped to a whisper.

"That is a family matter that does not concern you."

"Perhaps she doesn't think your money is as clean as you thought," Lyon said.

"It has nothing to do with money. It is a question of family honor, which she shamed. When I came in the door I saw them on the living room couch. They will be married as soon as the boy leaves the hospital."

"I'm arresting you," Rocco said.

Carillo waved a deprecating hand. "You have no power in Rhode Island. And if you did, you have nothing that my lawyers could not destroy."

"I am making a citizen's arrest for child abuse," Rocco said. "The evidence is in your home."

Carillo laughed. "I did what had to be done. The way it has always been done. You dumb cop! I've had experts try and get me—local cops, state cops, FBI, Senate committees, the Attorney General tried RICO, extortion, murder. Ha! You and your kiddie stuff. Get out of my restaurant!"

Rocco's hand closed over Carillo's wrist and squeezed until the man winced. "Come," Rocco said softly without threat.

"Tony!" Carillo managed to yell before Rocco shoved him through the front door.

Grumpy ejected through the kitchen doors and was halfway through the room before he hesitated and stopped. Carillo gave a snort and stopped struggling against Rocco's grip.

Bea Wentworth felt grouchy. This was an unusual state of mind for her. The usual cures, a shower, good coffee, and the Sunday crossword puzzle did not help. Their Sunday mornings were usually a placid time, lazily occupied with coffee and buns eaten while they sorted through the bulky *New York Times.* The day's woes had multiplied: the puzzle's topic had been puns and anagrams, her nemesis, they had inadvertently run out of coffee beans and were relegated to instant, and the buns were somehow stale. The combination was too much for good cheer, and had led to her present state of grouchiness.

Lyon wasn't helping matters any. When he sensed her foul mood, he had insisted on preparing his "special omelet." His preoccupation caused him to stand at the butcher's block chopping one onion into finer and smaller pieces as he stared off into space.

"That's not dicing," she said. "You're manufacturing quarks."

"You're right," he said and continued cutting the pieces even smaller. "Why isn't Carillo concerned about his men or the money?"

"Because they are his men," she snapped. "They worked for him all along and he has his money with interest." She scraped the onion from the block and replaced it with a slice of ham.

Lyon continued chopping without noticing the replacement. "The State Police have put out APBs on Brumby and Stockton, and Rocco has personally talked to the Vegas and Atlantic City police."

She took a sip of instant coffee and grimaced. "Then it's now a police matter and we are out of it. Which leaves me with two questions. Where does this leave Pan, Sam, and Dice?"

"It's hard to believe that they're all part of a conspiracy."

"And two, what about Carillo's granddaughter?" she asked with interest.

"Carillo was released on five hundred dollars' bond, but children's services has stepped in. Rocco says that maybe the FBI or Attorney General can't get Carillo, but he's never delt with real troublemakers like social workers."

"You guys did all you could." She stared out the window at the overgrown grass. "Have we decided to turn our lawn into an African savanna?"

"I had to avoid certain areas last time I mowed," Lyon said. "There was a family of rabbits by the pines, and some woodchucks were working near the garden, so I certainly couldn't mow there."

"And deer have probably taken up by the shed," she said. "It's animal eviction time. Thumper has to go." She marched out of the kitchen and across the lawn to the small shed where they kept the sit-down mower and other lawn tools. She was a staunch feminist who believed in complete equality between the sexes. She was more than willing to stand on a bus, or to have men snap doors in her face, but she still maintained two last vestiges of Fifties baggage. Men took out the garbage and did the grass. She was perfectly willing to shingle the roof, replace plumbing, or do wallpaper, but garbage and grass were strictly male domains. It suited her present state of mind to do grass as a self-inflicted punishment for her poor mood.

She squinted in the bright mid-morning sun, and snapped off the latch on the shed door and stepped into its dark interior. The instant change from bright sun to dim interior radically reduced her vision. A board squeaked under her foot as she reached toward the seat of the mower.

The figure in the stocking mask catapulted over the mower. Two powerful hands reached for her throat.

She was shoved harshly back against the wall. The door frame caused a sharp pain in the small of her back. The hands closed over her throat. It was becoming difficult to breathe. She thought she could feel his fetid breath against her face. She was gasping for her life.

She tried to break the strong grip at her neck. Her fingers rasped against the rough texture of heavy gloves. During an inappropriate minisecond, she recalled that she needed a new pair of gardening gloves herself.

She tore her right hand away from the killing grip, and scratched it across the wall of the shed by her side. Her fingers closed tightly over the handle of a tool, and she swung the implement in a wide arc that fell across her attacker's back. She struck again, and then again. The pressure on her neck loosened as her attacker recoiled.

Bea swung the weapon again. As it passed across the door opening, sunlight glinted from the razor-edge blade of the hand scythe.

Her attacker rose before her. Bea screamed and with both hands swung the scythe directly at the figure's neck.

A severed head rolled across the shed floor. Bea screamed again and stumbled from the shed. She knelt in the grass with retching gasps.

Lyon, holding a kitchen utensil, ran across the yard toward her.

She looked down at her hands still gripping the deadly scythe, and she let the weapon fall to the ground. She had just decapitated a man, and her husband was running to her rescue carrying a spatula.

13

They stood in front of the shed and looked at the body. The head had fallen in the shadows within the shed, and Lyon stepped across the threshold to lift it by the stocking mask and throw it out on the lawn where it rolled to a stop by Bea's feet. "At least it was a relatively bloodless slaying," Lyon said as he kicked the torso.

"That's not funny," she said.

He went back inside the shed to squat near the floor. He ran his fingers over certain objects he found there, and then returned to sit beside her on the grass. "It was triggered by a spring under the loose floorboard. It was mounted over the mower so that when released it came right at whoever was standing near the door."

She picked up the head. "It was dark. I thought someone was killing me, and I cut off his head."

"Without the stocking mask, it looks like one of those dummies they use for automobile testing. When it jumped out at you in the dark, you had no way of knowing he wasn't real."

"And you rushed to my rescue with a spatula. Were you going to turn him over easy? Couldn't you have at least grabbed a butcher knife?"

Lyon looked at her in mock horror. "And be a party to a beheading?"

"Thanks a pile."

He pulled her gently to her feet and led her toward the house. "Let's leave this whole mess. I'll take you to the Murphysville Inn for one of their famous Sunday brunches complete with an extra-strong Bloody Mary."

"With that in mind, my disposition has already begun to improve. I know it's not nice to speak ill of the dead, but that rat fink Dalton set up that trick before he left."

For three hundred years the Murphysville Inn had either been a stagecoach stop or inn. It sat on a small hill above the river on the outskirts of town. The Murphysville Yacht Club's rustic clubhouse and boat slips were at the base of the hill. The inn offered lodgings in a dozen antiques-furnished rooms above the restaurant, and the dining facilities included the Forge Room, the Bar Room, or the larger dining area known as the Taproom. The ceilings were low, and the walls were covered with Currier and Ives lithographs. The food was plain generic New England, and the prices were high.

On Sundays, a long table was installed in the Taproom laden with warming dishes of eggs, breads, hams, and turkeys.

Lyon asked for a table by the window in the Forge Room, and their Bloody Marys were quickly served. Bea drank with gratitude. "The day is already looking a mite better."

"Pandora is the one who put a microphone in our box springs," Lyon said.

"Is that a non sequitur?" she asked.

"I'm trying to imagine who else in the world would pull a trick like the lunging strangler. It required a good deal of strength to set the springs on that dummy," Lyon said.

A pitcher of Bloody Marys was put on the table. Bea looked across the room to see the inn's owner, a distinguished, white-haired man, standing in the room's archway. He waved and mouthed the word "compliments" to her.

"I think it was rigged by Dalton," Lyon continued.

"The day was improving, Went, don't spoil it."

"I was in that shed two days ago," Lyon said. "Nothing sprang out at me then. The dummy was rigged within the last forty-eight hours."

"You saw Dalton dead on Red Deer Island before the fire. He was hanging, if you will recall."

"I saw him dead in our living room a few days before that, but he was resurrected."

Bea poured another Bloody Mary. "Now we're into the occult."

"How about sleight of hand instead?"

"Did you see him hanging?"

"Yes, I did."

"Then finish your drink, and don't spoil my enjoyment of the buffet."

A wheelchair, pushed by a nondescript man in a dark suit, appeared in the archway. The chair's occupant had a robe tucked around his lower body, but his torso was clothed in an Oscar de la Renta tailored suit. The patient had an extremely large head topped with a wave of yellowing hair. His facial features were accentuated by deep craggy lines. His left arm and the left side of his face were rigid and frozen, the result of a stroke. Lyon watched with interest as the man with the interesting face was pushed to a table across the room.

"The man in the wheelchair looks familiar," Lyon said.

Bea took a quick glance at the other table. "I met him on my last visit to the Murphysville Convalescent Hospital. His name is . . ." She searched her memory. "Lawrence Thorndike. I believe he was a stage actor before he had a stroke and retired."

"I must have seen him in some play."

The deep and sonorous voice carried clearly across the room. "I do not want juice, Melvin. I do not want a Shirley Temple. I want a goddamn strong martini."

Bea covered the lower part of her face with her hand to hide the smile. "I think they told me he was nearly ninety."

"I hope I want a drink when I'm ninety," Lyon said. "That voice is familiar, but I don't identify it with a Broadway play. It was something I heard as a kid. Larry Lash!" Lyon raised his voice so that it boomed across the room. "There's trouble on the prairie tonight!"

"But Larry Lash on Flyer will ride!" the actor's sonorous voice returned with equal volume.

At the archway, the inn's owner held up his hands in a plea for quiet.

"Get over here, young fellow," the actor called to Lyon.

"Bring your drink," Lyon said to Bea as he pushed back from the table. Bea picked up her glass, looked at the nearly full pitcher, and took that also.

After introductions, they sat at the Thorndike table. "Not many remember Larry Lash," the actor said. "Made a hundred of those damn things. I went out to Hollywood in thirty when they needed voices. Never been on a horse except for carriage rides around Central Park with a little slap and tickle with some ingenue. We made those Larry Lashes in a week. Used to see them on the TV in the Fifties. Terrible."

"I heard you did some stage work for O'Neill, Mr. Thorndike," Bea said.

"Sure in hell did. Joined them when the Provincetown Players moved to New York. Now you take Gene. He was a real man's drinker. Mean son of a bitch when drunk, but a hell of a writer when sober. I played with the Lunts in *The Guardsman*, great actors those two."

"Do you remember the movie, *Guns at Gut Creek?*" Lyon asked.

"Can't say that I do," Thorndike answered. "All those damn things were alike, and sometimes we made them up as we went along."

"*Guns at Gut Creek* starts out with a sheepherder getting hanged for rustling cattle."

"Did Larry Lash say there was trouble on the prairie tonight?"

"You always said that line in all those movies, Grandfather," his companion said.

"Who'd you say got hanged?"

"A sheepherder."

"Hell, son, I know that. Sheepmen always got the short end, but who played the part? I might recall it."

Lyon thought a moment. "Harry Carey. Harry Carey Senior, that is. It was a small part, but he had some good lines when he had to write a last letter to his little girl and told her that he'd meet her in the great-prairie-in-the-sky."

"Hell, yes. I remember it. Only time I ever worked with Harry. He became a great character actor in his later years."

"There's a scene where they slap Harry's horse and the

rope tightens around his neck, and well, he's hanged. How do they do that?"

"You mean how they hanged him? There's no big trick to that. They put a waist harness under his shirt, and from that a wire runs up the back and through the center of the rope and around the tree limb. It looks good, but he's not really hanging at all. Which makes it refill time. I need another martini, and make it a double this time."

Bea had just finished mixing a huge batch of Bloody Marys when she realized that they had never eaten the inn's buffet. In fact, they hadn't eaten anything all day. As soon as they had left Thorndike's table, Lyon had made several phone calls on the inn's phone and then rushed her to the car for a fast drive back to Nutmeg Hill.

Rocco Herbert now straddled a chair on the patio with a drink of straight vodka in his hand. Captain Norbert, dressed in what he perceived as a Scottish golfing outfit, waited impatiently for his drink. He did not appear pleased. A diminutive man sat uncomfortably in a chair near the parapet. He was so short that his feet barely touched the ground. He was dressed in a suit that Bea was convinced had to have been purchased at a department store's prep shop.

Lyon took the pitcher from Bea and poured drinks for everyone except Rocco, who replenished his own.

"I want to thank you for coming, Doctor Mellin," Lyon said.

"Senator Wentworth has always been most supportive of the Medical Examiner's office," Mellin replied in a voice that was in keeping with his stature.

Captain Norbert tapped his glass on the edge of the parapet. "Can we get this moving along, Wentworth? I'm scheduled to play golf with the major today."

Doctor Mellin giggled. "One good thing about my job is that the patients are never in a hurry."

"And never pay their bills," Norbert said and guffawed at his own joke.

"I hope what you've turned up is important," Rocco said.

"Something happened to us this morning that I consider significant," Lyon said. "Specifically, it happened to Bea when she went out to the shed to start the mower." He told them in detail about the incident of the attacking mannequin. They were silent when he finished. Rocco looked bemused. Doctor Mellin looked puzzled, as if waiting for the punch line. Captain Norbert looked annoyed.

"Let me get this straight," Norbert finally said. "You probably want Rocco, as the local police chief, to give you protection. You want Doctor Mellin to autopsy your dummy, and me to get a State Police SWAT team looking for marauding mannequins. Come on now."

"I know of only one person in this state who concocts elaborate tricks of that nature," Lyon said levelly.

"It could have been set up weeks ago," Rocco added.

"I was in that shed two days ago and nothing happened then," Lyon said.

"Jesus, Wentworth, lots of people play jokes," Norbert said. "It could have been set by anyone. Dalton Turman is dead. Do you understand, dead?" He bounced his glass on the stone parapet and it shattered in his hand. He looked down at the pieces in surprise.

Lyon replaced the captain's drink. "Another thing," Lyon went on. "Dalton was in bed with loan sharks, and yet remarkably they are suddenly not interested in repayment of their money."

"They're pragmatists," Rocco said. "You can't collect from a dead man, and their kind of debt isn't one you can pursue against an estate."

Norbert shrugged. "So, what do you suggest?"

"That the money's been paid back."

"Pan could have done it to get them off her back. She had life insurance money in addition to the fifty thousand that Bea discovered," Rocco said.

"I think Dalton is alive," Lyon said.

"Oh, my God," Norbert said and nearly broke his second glass. "What in the hell have you been smoking? You identified the body. You described how he had been tortured and then hanged. You saw him."

"We learned this morning that there's a way to hang without being hurt," Bea said.

"I cut somebody up," Doctor Mellin stated categorically. "Say what you will, there was a man's body on my table, and we did him up right."

"Granted that the practical joke this morning was quirky," Rocco said, "and I can imagine that it's possible to fake a hanging, but if that didn't kill him, the fire sure in hell did."

"Death was by asphyxiation prior to any possibility of smoke inhalation," the Medical Examiner said with quiet authority. "I would stake my career on that."

"Okay," Rocco continued, "you not only saw the body, but we identified the fingerprints from the finger in the box."

"There was a definite match between that finger and the army files the FBI had on Mr. Turman. In addition, his wife identified the wedding ring on the finger," Mellin said smugly, as if pleased to make his contribution.

"One print off one finger is all we need, Wentworth," Captain Norbert said. "Prints don't lie. They never have and they never will."

"Was a match made between the severed finger and the cadaver's hand?" Lyon asked. "Was a microscopic examination made to determine if the finger's severed bone matched the hand?"

The Medical Examiner looked thunderstruck. "Under the circumstances of identification, such tests did not seem warranted."

"What about the teeth?" Lyon asked.

"Teeth! I'm always getting teeth!" Doctor Mellin seemed to be getting more and more agitated. "There is no central registry for teeth, you know. To compare physical dental work with the records, we have to know who the victim might be and who the dentist was. The decedent's wife did not know his dentist. I understand they had only been married a few months, and there did not seem to be any reason to pursue that avenue further."

"We can get a court order to exhume the body," Bea said.

Mellin downed the remainder of his drink and poured himself another while he shook his head. "The body was released to the wife and was cremated."

"That's bad luck," Lyon said, "but I understand that fluid analysis is very sophisticated these days. We might be able to at least exclude Dalton's identity."

"Dumped," Mellin said as he drank.

"What?"

"You were all so hot to have a fast report that we did our work, released the body, and destroyed the examined organs and fluids," the doctor said. "Our files are closed."

"As a matter of curiosity, who do you think we found out there?" Rocco asked.

"Considering everything, including relative size," Lyon said, "I believe it was one of the men who worked for Carillo, the one called Stockton."

"Then what happened to the other one?" Rocco asked.

"I expect that he is also dead."

"Killed by Dalton Turman," Norbert snorted.

"Probably."

Norbert stood with feet apart and arms akimbo. "All this crap is because someone played a joke on you two this morning."

"That's how it started," Lyon said. "But everything fits if you assume that Dalton is alive."

"Which would mean that he was the one who killed Katrina Loops," Rocco said. "Probably because she knew too much."

"We have arrested a man who the court saw fit to place under three hundred thousand dollars bond for that killing," Norbert said. "When he goes to trial, we are going to nail his hide to the wall."

"It's the wrong man," Bea said as she poured Doctor Mellin another drink.

"I've had it!" Norbert shouted. "Do you know how much trouble you cause me, Wentworth? Whenever you get involved in police business you cause trouble. You shot a cop, for Christ's sake. You are also either a nut, incompetent, or drunk. And that's exactly what this conversation sounds like. You are a bunch of bored people sitting around a patio on a Sunday afternoon drinking too many Bloody Marys and creating nutty ideas about corpses that come alive. You are a bunch of professional drinkers who think they're amateur detectives."

"I resent that," Bea said as she hiccupped.

Doctor Mellin stumbled forward with raised fists. "You can't talk to Senator Wentworth that way." He rushed at Captain Norbert, and when the police officer stepped aside, the Medical Examiner fell over the parapet and disappeared from view.

"I think this party is deteriorating," Rocco said.

"And we know about you, Herbert," Norbert said. "You are a proven drunk who sees snakes. God only knows what Wentworth sees."

"Would you believe furry animals with long snouts and beady little eyes?" Bea laughed.

"I believe it. God, do I believe it," Norbert said as he stalked from the patio. "And to think I could have been playing golf with the major and letting him cheat a little," they heard him say as he left slamming the front door.

"Someone ought to see if the Medical Examiner is dead," Rocco said. "Because if he is, we have a real problem of who to call."

Lyon squinted into the early-morning sunlight streaming through the bedroom window. He groaned and tweaked Bea's big toe that protruded from under the sheet. She groaned. He searched the room and picked up dropped clothing from various locations and pulled on khaki pants, a sport shirt, and slipped into topsiders. When he went downstairs he passed the living room where Rocco's long frame overlapped the couch. The coffee had almost finished perking when the front door opened.

Martha Herbert, followed by her daughter, Remley, stalked into the living room. She threw a handful of clothes at Rocco. Their daughter dropped a shaving kit on his head. The large police chief moaned and sat up as Lyon sank a coffee mug into his hand.

"Good morning, dear," Rocco said to his wife.

"She's not speaking to you," his daughter replied.

"I called last night and told you that I was working on a case," Rocco mumbled.

"A case of vodka," Martha snorted before she retraced her stalk back to her car.

"This is another example of the decadent idle rich taking advantage of the working class," Remley said. "Once again the bourgeois have seduced the workers by enticing them with grape in order to close their eyes against the inequalities of the system." She glanced at her father once more before following her mother to the car.

"That's got a nice ring to it," Bea said as she shuffled into the kitchen.

"I didn't know we were that decadent," Lyon said as he poured coffee for Bea.

"We absolutely drink too much."

"And I didn't know we were rich."

"I know for a fact that's untrue," Bea said.

"I never really think about money, there always seems to be enough."

"That's your problem, Went. People who aren't rich should always think a lot about money."

"You've got to do something for me," Lyon said.

"Don't ask much. I'm not up to it. Thank God the Senate's not in session today."

"I want you to keep the Medical Examiner here all day. I don't want him to have any phone calls or contact with anyone."

"How am I supposed to do that?" Bea asked. "Seduction?"

"He has a liquor capacity of exactly one drink. It shouldn't be too difficult."

"Everything's going to be difficult today," Rocco said as he entered the kitchen and leaned against the wall.

"I'd like you to come with me," Lyon said to Rocco. "I need you to follow Pan after I give her certain information."

"What information?" Bea asked.

"That Doctor Mellin has discovered that the body wasn't Dalton's."

"Come on, Lyon, that's a lie, and you are one hell of a bad liar," Bea said.

"Not when I really believe what I'm saying."

Doctor Mellin, immaculately groomed and looking

none the worse for wear, entered and smiled at them. "Thank you so much for a wonderful time. I really must run."

Lyon went quickly to the refrigerator and poured a large glass half full of fresh orange juice. With his back to the others except Rocco, he laced the drink with a large dollop of vodka. "Please have some juice before you rush off," he said to the doctor as he handed him the glass.

Doctor Mellin gratefully took the juice and drank almost all of it. "I feel so terrible that I'd kill myself except that Barton would do the autopsy, and he does such sloppy work. Do you know, I'm feeling better already." He drank the remainder of the juice. "In fact, I think I'll have another, if that's all right?" Lyon prepared another spiked OJ as Mellin plunked a small radio device on the table. "I found this in the room and tried to tune in the news this morning. Dumb of me, it seems to be some sort of ham radio."

"So much for my housekeeping," Bea said as she picked up Pan's receiving device. "I thought she had taken it with her."

"Where's the bug we found in the mattress?" Lyon asked.

"In the middle kitchen drawer," Bea said.

Lyon searched the drawer until he found the transmitter and pocketed it along with the receiver.

"I could use one of those orange juices," Rocco said.

"We have to go," Lyon answered as he dragged Rocco from the room.

The Medical Examiner raised his glass in a toast to their departure.

14

The police cruiser swerved out of the driveway and rocked violently on its shocks when it hit the highway straightaway. Rocco flipped on the dome lights and siren as he increased speed to ninety.

"I think you're teed off about something," Lyon said as both hands frantically clutched the dashboard.

"I wanted some of that orange juice you were feeding the ME." The cruiser fishtailed as they cornered and Rocco momentarily fought for control.

"If you don't kill us in the next five minutes, we have a lot to do today."

Rocco gave him a grumpy look but did switch off the

siren as he reduced speed to a saner fifty. "You have it all wrong. Within the incorporated city limits of Murphysville, I am in charge of all police activity. You are a civilian, subject to my orders in all matters concerning crime, investigations, and keeping the peace. Is that understood?"

"Of course."

"All right then, what are we going to do?"

"I am going to talk to Pan and plant the bug in her cottage. You will listen, and also keep her under surveillance from a spot on top of Malvern Hill."

As Lyon walked through the entrance, he could see that the resort had been rejuvenated. Men were back at work, new deliveries of construction material had been made, and there was an aura of renewed vitality. He stopped before the door to Pan's cottage and looked over his shoulder. On a small rise in the distance, he could barely see Rocco's cruiser through the foliage. He knocked on the door.

"The door's unlocked. Just leave the groceries on the table," a muffled feminine voice said from the interior.

He stepped into the living room and was surprised at the amount of cartons piled four and five high throughout the small room. A shower, barely audible over the strains of rock music, could be heard in the bathroom located off the bedroom. He quickly flipped open the lids of several unsealed cartons. They seemed to contain a great many books, picture albums, and photography equipment, along with a mundane collection of ordinary household goods.

He slipped the tiny transmitter bug from his pocket and unscrewed the mouthpiece of the telephone receiver. He attached the bug inside and rescrewed the lid. The device would not only pick up phone conversation, but would transmit ordinary room conversation.

Pan walked into the room wearing a towel turban and nothing else. She gave a gasp when she saw him and retreated back into the bedroom. "My God, I thought the delivery boy had left."

"Sorry," Lyon shouted to her.

The door opened a crack and she peered at him through the aperture. "What do you want, Wentworth?"

"All these boxes really clutter up the place," Lyon said.

"I was moving everything from the house Dalton sold to the boat, but never had a chance to finish."

"That was convenient," Lyon said.

She stepped back into the room. "Yeah, I'm a real lucky widow to have all my mementos." She was still nude, and walked provocatively to an end table and picked up a package of cigarettes. She slowly lit one and exhaled. "Seen enough?"

He didn't answer.

"You may as well make a move. You already got blamed for it anyway." She pushed a box to the side and sat on it. "Well?"

He looked into her eyes, but they stared back at him without revelation. "Well, what?"

"Why in the hell are you here?"

"I will always be beholden to Dalton for saving my life. You are the only way I can communicate with him."

"I never learned how to talk with the dead, sorry."

"Dalton's alive."

She mashed her cigarette out on the floor in a violent gesture. "That's not funny. It's mean and sadistic."

"Rocco Herbert is a good friend of mine, and he's related to Captain Norbert of the State Police. They told me, in strictest confidence, that the Medical Examiner has come up with positive proof that the body we identified is not Dalton."

"That's impossible! I saw Dalton's wedding ring. It was

the one I gave him. You saw him on the boat. What kind of game is this? What are you trying to do to me?"

"It occurred to me that this might be very important information for Dalton. Call it interest on my debt."

"I don't believe you. This is some kind of get-Pan game."

"They have the evidence even after cremation."

"You're ticked off because I told your wife we made it together. You snickering bastard, I have a death certificate. The insurance company has paid death benefits. You were the one who put everything together."

"And now the Medical Examiner is taking it all apart." Lyon ticked off points on his fingers. "One, the Medical Examiner attempted to match the severed finger to the hand on the cadaver. It did not fit, Pandora. It was not from the same body."

She held both hands to her face as if obliterating his image would stop him from continuing. "They released the body to me."

"Two: a lab analysis of the body fluids exclude Dalton."

"They told me it was Dalton."

"In haste, and before completion of the other tests. The Medical Examiner takes full responsibility, but claims we pressured him for results before he completed the work on the body fluids and X-ray examinations."

"This is crazy."

"You have to come to terms with the fact that Dalton is alive."

She unraveled the turban and threw the towel into a corner. She shook her head until blond hair cascaded over her shoulders. A lock fell over the side of her face and partially covered one eye. Veronica Lake, Lyon thought, and wondered why such movie trivia sprang to mind. She haphazardly ran her hand through her hair. It was a transparent subterfuge to gain time.

"The body might not be his, but he could still be dead somewhere else," she said.

"That's possible."

"Or he could be a prisoner."

"That too."

"Or you could just like talking to naked ladies," she said in one of her strange, abrupt emotional shifts.

"As a matter of fact, I find it disconcerting," Lyon said. "I noticed that you have a good many photographs in some of those boxes. I know Dalton liked to have a picture record of his pranks . . . do you have any that show him hanging in a harness?"

"I don't know that trick," she said slowly. "It might have been one he did before we met." She crossed to a cluttered chair where she put on a rumpled white blouse and buttoned the two middle buttons. After a sly look at Lyon, she ripped open the blouse. "I'm going to scream rape in about two seconds, duck butter. You had better get your ass out of here, because when I yell, I yell loud."

"My message was for Dalton," Lyon said as he left the small cottage and the naked woman who looked after him with such hate in her eyes.

"She phoned the Medical Examiner's office as soon as you were out the door," Rocco said as Lyon got into the car and leaned back against the seat cushions.

"Did she scream that I attacked her?"

"Not yet. I didn't think you were in an attacking mood this morning."

"I'm not, but that doesn't discourage her. What did she say to the ME's office?"

"She wanted to know where in the hell he was and why the report on Dalton was changed. Naturally, no one in the office knew what she was talking about. She ended up yelling mean words at them. That little Southern lady has really got a foul mouth on her."

"Tell me about it."

"What now?"

"Can you radio for a car to take me to my next stop?" Lyon asked.

"While I sit here and watch her?"

"Something like that," Lyon said. "Do you mind?"

Rocco sighed. "Does it matter?"

Rocco Herbert wondered how many years of his life had been spent sitting in cars watching for other cars, or looking at store fronts, houses of all descriptions, woods, sewer culverts, school yards, or a bunch of other strange locales. He'd had enough foresight to ask the driver of the car who picked up Lyon to bring a container of coffee and a couple of large meatball grinders. The grinders were messy to eat but helped to pass the time.

Pan Turman made several more calls to the Medical Examiner's office until the receptionist recognized her voice and hung up before the yelling began. Another call had been made to the State Police barracks, where she was informed that Norbert had taken a personal discretion day and was probably on the golf course. There were three calls to his own office, and luckily each time she was informed that he was still out in the field. Thank God for small favors, he thought. It was a wonder that his communications clerk hadn't informed her that the chief was on a surveillance of the Turman cottage at the Pincus resort.

No one had entered the cottage. He yawned and belched a regret at the grinders. It was late afternoon when Pan opened the cottage door and stepped outside. She started up the walk, and then, as if subliminally warned, retreated back inside. She had been wearing jeans and a T-shirt, and Rocco wondered what had spooked her.

At dusk he would have to move the car. His sight lines would be obscured, and it would be necessary to actually drive onto the resort property and park in the shadows of a building nearer her cottage.

The sound of the start of a powerful engine startled him. He glanced around without seeing a moving vehicle, and then snapped binoculars to his eyes. "You little bitch!" he said aloud. She had outsmarted him.

The sleek cigarette boat, with 400 horse under its long inboard canopy, darted from the pier behind the cottage and turned in a long sweep that would carry it toward the open waters of Long Island Sound. Rocco's binoculars gave him a quick glimpse of Pan, hunched intently over the controls, as she guided the powerful craft.

He should have had water backup, he thought. He pounded the steering wheel in frustration. "Damn!"

The uniformed male clerk looked at Lyon with opaque eyes. "You heard me, buddy. Three hundred thousand dollars. This ain't no bazaar, we don't bargain and haggle over price. So, take it or leave it."

"In other words, if I kill several people and bail is set at a million dollars, and I happen to have a million, I can leave here without spending a day in jail?"

"If the judge sets bail, and you got the scratch, you walk."

"If I hold up a convenience store," Lyon said, "and I don't have twenty thousand for bail, I could wait in jail for a year or two until my trial." He was answered by a cold stare that signified that the clerk divided the world into two parts, those that were either in jail, going to jail, or leaving jail; and the other half of the population who were the designated keepers.

"That's the deal, buddy. You want to make bail, or you want to talk judicial philosophy?"

"I don't have a choice."

"Not if you want your buddy out of the slammer, you don't."

It was another half an hour before Bobby Douglas was led into the Correction Center anteroom where Lyon waited. One half of his face was covered with a bluish-purple bruise, and a long cut ran down the other cheek. "What happened?" Lyon asked.

"I'll tell you about being in jail, Mr. Wentworth—never play Ping-Pong with seven-foot guys who hate to lose."

Bea looked puzzled, but she automatically smiled and shook hands with Bobby Douglas. "They must have dropped your case, Bobby?" she said.

"Not yet, but the public defender says that if I plead to manslaughter, she can get me off with a seven-to-life. I can't tell you how much I appreciate Lyon putting up bail for me. I was going ape in that place."

She looked at Lyon. "I put up my half of Nutmeg Hill," he said in answer to her unspoken question.

"You did what?"

"I put up my half . . ."

"That was a rhetorical, you did what? Do you realize that if Bobby takes off, the State of Connecticut gets half the house? That means that I would share a dwelling with the Governor, who would then become my significant other."

"Gee, Mrs. Wentworth, I'll be back as soon as I play in the Dublin Doubles," Bobby said with a smile.

"Can't we slash his Achilles tendon?" Bea suggested.

"Put your things in the guest room at the top of the stairs," Lyon said to Bobby.

Lyon mixed Bea a martini and poured a Dry Sack sherry

for himself while Douglas took a leisurely shower and changed. "By the way," he called to Bea on the patio, "Bobby is not allowed to leave the state, and what happened to Doctor Mellin?"

"He was retrieved by his wife about three this afternoon. She tells me that at home, she doesn't even allow him to have rum cake or use shaving lotion."

Lyon answered the phone with one hand while gently stirring martinis with the other. Rocco succinctly told him about Pan's evasion of his surveillance, and described the speedboat in detail. Lyon thanked him and went out on the patio.

"Did you know that Dalton bought something called a cigarette boat for the resort?" Lyon asked Douglas when he came downstairs.

"Sure. He asked my advice on what sort of speedboat to get, and I suggested a couple of models. He wouldn't have any part of my ideas. He had to have something that had power. I never could figure it, that thing was too fast to pull water-skiers, much less take old ladies sight-seeing. It was better suited for shooting torpedoes at aircraft carriers than as a launch for a resort."

"Or maybe to run cargo from a mother ship," Bea said.

"Yeah," Bobby agreed. "You see a lot of them in Florida, and that's exactly what they're used for."

"Speaking of boats, Bobby," Lyon said. "What sort of dinghy did the houseboat have?"

"It was designed to pull a launch, but he hadn't gotten one yet. There was a small runabout lashed on the roof."

Lyon remembered the small boat stored behind the bridge. "Did it have a motor?"

"A small outboard."

"Tell me its speed and range," Lyon said.

"It had two hours' time with a full tank, but you could

always carry a spare five gallons and increase the range. The top speed was maybe seven or eight miles an hour."

"Interesting," Lyon said.

"Did it ever occur to you that you are still operating without any hard information?" Bea asked.

"Pan ran," Lyon said. "She went to warn Dalton."

"That's ridiculous!"

"Is it?" Rocco said from the doorway. He took the small radio transmitter from his pocket and centered it on the patio table. "The message started a few minutes ago. Listen."

They stared at the transmitter as Rocco turned the volume as high as it would go.

"I know you're out there somewhere, Wentworth. Sooner or later you will hear this and know that Prankenstein has struck again. Guess who?"

The laughter was unmistakably Dalton Turman's.

15

The message transmitted over the small receiver continued, "My only regret is that I don't have a picture of the look on your face. It was thoughtful of you to plant the bug in such an obvious place. It made this message easy to transmit. But enough, let us meet at the resort ballroom at seven tonight. I have recorded this message and it will be repeated." The message ended, and for a few moments all they could hear was static, until it started again. "I know you're out there somewhere, Wentworth . . ." Rocco snapped it off.

"He's got to be kidding," Bobby Douglas said as he lurched from his chair and rushed toward the door. Rocco grabbed his arm. "Let me go! I'm going to kill the son of a bitch!"

"There goes the family homestead," Bea said.

"Keep this guy here," Rocco ordered. "I've got to get down to the office and start the paperwork. It's going to take a hell of a long time just to type up the warrants."

"Warrants for what?" Lyon asked.

"I'm going to start with page one of the felony statutes and keep going until I have a fistful of charges against Dalton. It's going to take me a while to sort it out," Rocco said, "but all that I know is that Dalton didn't just cross over the line, he obliterated it, and I'm going to crucify him."

Willey P. Lynch, attorney-at-law, had a physique constructed in concentric circles like the preliminary body sketches drawn by cartoonists. His head, torso, and lower body were, if not circular, at least elliptical in shape. Many years ago he had decided that his girth could not be camouflaged, and had discarded any pretense of dress that did not accentuate his proportions. His suits were dark, and he always wore a garish gold chain that looped down his vest and over the protrusion of his stomach. His complete lack of hair did not disturb the symmetry.

He considered himself the Friar Tuck of litigators, except that his mission in life was not limited to cudgels with the Sheriff of Nottingham, but to battles with all the sheriffs in all the jurisdictions. "The great defense attorneys are leaving the field of battle, and therefore we must fight harder," he periodically announced to new associates when they joined his firm. "The Percy Foremans and the Clarence Darrowes are gone, but we shall lift the banner and carry it forward." Sometimes the younger lawyers smiled at these remarks, in which instance their tenure was short.

Willey had never lost a criminal case in open court, although he would sometimes secretly admit to resorting to some creative plea bargaining prior to trial.

He glanced at his newest client sitting across the table in the ballroom of the Pincus resort. Willey nodded appreciatively. It was going to be an interesting case with future legal skirmishes that could be savored in anticipation. "You understand that I guarantee nothing?" he said softly to Dalton. "However, there is one small matter . . ."

Dalton smiled and handed the cashier's check across the table. Willey made a tiny gesture at his young associate sitting by his side who immediately took the check. "I count on your reputation," Dalton said.

"Do you have the writs?" Willey asked his associate.

Doris Lemming grimly patted the attaché case on the table in front of her. "All properly executed and signed," she said.

Willey nodded. He knew they would be. Doris was ruthlessly efficient. He sometimes thought she hated men, in fact she often appeared to hate everyone. She had many of the attributes of a shark or a large predatory cat. She was a ruthless, verbal killing machine. She would make a great litigator.

Rocco Herbert was the first one through the wide doors that led to the ballroom. He did not break stride or glance to the right or left as he headed toward the table where Dalton sat with his lawyers. Handcuffs were in his right hand by the time he arrived at the table.

Dalton reached out to shake Rocco's hand and the cuffs were snapped over his wrist. Rocco deftly spun him and snapped a cuff on the other wrist. "Your manners are terrible, Rocco."

"Man, I'd put you in a net with leg irons if it wasn't against regulations," Rocco said.

"We are not in your jurisdiction, Chief Herbert," Willey said mildly.

For the first time Rocco seemed to take note of Willey's presence. "Oh, Christ, Lynch, are you involved in this?"

"Of course. And we were talking of your powers to arrest in other areas."

"I have the powers necessary to arrest anywhere when I am in hot pursuit. And by God, I *am* in hot pursuit." He turned to start dragging Dalton toward the door. "You have the right to remain silent. You have . . ."

Willey slowly stood with his palm extended toward Doris. She immediately slapped a folded legal paper into his hand like a scrub nurse passing a surgical instrument. "Chief Herbert," Willey called, "this is for you." He handed the paper to Rocco.

Rocco looked at it in astonishment. "A writ?"

"You are hereby ordered to refrain from doing what you are presently doing, that is, arresting Dalton Turman."

"He hasn't even been booked yet."

"Please honor the judge's order and release him immediately. You know me well enough to realize that I stand on firm legal ground."

Rocco slowly opened the handcuffs. "I will be at the prosecuting attorney's office first thing in the morning to obtain warrants."

"We shall see," Willey smiled. "Now sit down, Chief, and I will explain Mr. Turman's position in detail when the others arrive."

Lyon and Bea had observed the confrontation from the doorway. They watched as André, the caterer, hovered deferentially over Dalton and Willey with an open order pad. Sam Idelweise and Randolph Dice were huddled at a small table in the corner engaged in a hushed and conspiratorial conversation. A bartender had appeared at the long bar, which now ran along one wall, and was making his final preparations for cocktail orders.

"A pony of Dry Sack for Mr. Wentworth and a very dry vodka martini for Senator Wentworth," Dalton told André, who scurried over to the bar with his orders.

"What do you say at a time like this?" Bea whispered to Lyon. "Glad you're back from the dead, when are your visiting days in prison, or how did you do it, you crumb?"

"Some from column A and some from B," Lyon said. They sat at a table with Rocco, two removed from Dalton and the lawyers.

"Don't turn around," Rocco said, "but there are a couple of guys on the patio wearing combat fatigues and flak jackets. I do believe Norbie has arrived with his backup SWAT team. If he kicks in the door, I am going to throw up."

Captain Norbert of the State Police kicked in the door with the aid of two corporals who carried army assault weapons. Norbert advanced toward Dalton in a shooting crouch, while his backup took firing positions on either side.

"Please don't say freeze," Rocco said under his breath.

"Everyone freeze!" Norbert commanded.

"I wish he hadn't said that," Rocco said as he clinked the ice in his empty glass until it was replenished by a hovering waiter.

"We do have a writ for the State Police, do we not?" Willey asked.

"Yes, sir." Doris Lemming handed him the document.

"Captain Norbert," Willey said, "we have a paper for you executed by a sitting judge."

"What in the hell are you talking about, Lynch?" Norbert inched his hand toward the lawyer's while pointing his service revolver at Dalton. He took the writ in one hand, shook it loose, and glanced down at it. "Who signed this garbage? What drunken, senile judge do you have on your payroll this time, Willey?"

"My daddy," Doris Lemming said with a smile. "I'll tell him what a great fan you are next time we play golf with the major."

Willey P. Lynch looked at his associate with fresh awe.

She had the instincts of a cobra and the social graces of a vulture. For the first time in his career, he had potential partnership material at hand. "Who else are we expecting this evening?"

Doris examined her notes on a yellow legal pad. "The federal people are interested in Mr. Turman for a number of reasons, and other state agencies are still to be heard from."

"I'm representing all the state agencies," Norbert said. "And the feds were going to piggyback on my arrest." He held out his hand. "Hit me with the rest of the writs."

A man dressed in combat fatigues, with a belt of ammunition laced over his shoulders and carrying an M-60 machine gun, burst through the patio doors. He levered the bolt of the weapon and swept its barrel across the room. "You a hostage, Captain?"

"No, I'm not a goddamn hostage," Norbert said. "Tell everyone to take five."

The machine gunner looked puzzled. "Take a break during an assault?"

"Damn it! You heard me," Norbert snapped. "How does a guy get a drink around here?"

Dalton signaled André, who took the captain's order. "See what the troops outside will have," Dalton said.

The machine gunner ejected the belt of ammunition from his weapon and draped it around his neck. He stood the gun in a corner and ambled over to the bar. "I'd like a wine spritz," he said to the bartender.

"That's what I was telling you last week, Rocco," Norbert said. "In the old days it was beer and a shot, not wimpy wine, for Chrissake."

"Now that everyone's here, we can begin with Mr. Turman's explanation of certain recent events," Willey said.

"Am I late?" Pan Turman, dressed in a black cocktail dress with a scooped bodice, rushed breathlessly into the room.

"Show's just about to start," Dalton said as he pulled out a chair by his side.

Willey detested interruptions. "If I might begin?" He scowled pointedly at Pan. Dalton opened his mouth preparatory to speaking, but Willey placed his hand over it. "You, Mr. Turman, on my advice, will not say anything. You will not utter a single word, syllable, or even grunt comprehensible sounds." He stood and walked out in front of the tables. "As we all know, Mr. Turman has just returned from a harrowing experience. What all of you do not know, is that only through a magnificent display of great personal courage and a bit of luck was he able to escape from his abductor."

"I believe in the tooth fairy, too," Rocco said in a stage whisper.

"This prominent businessman, with no history of criminal activity except for some minor misdemeanors for mischievous mischief that we all laugh about . . ."

"Yeah, I split a gut over that carnage we thought was a mass murder," Norbert said and was the recipient of a glare from Willey.

"To continue," Willey said. "This entrepreneur who has contributed so much to this state and both political parties, was the victim of a heinous crime. He was asked by a friend in Rhode Island to provide employment for two recovering alcoholics. He was then kidnapped at gunpoint by the very men he had befriended." Willey began to pace as he became caught up in his presentation.

"Shakespeare said kill all the lawyers," Bea whispered to Lyon.

"One of the tasks Mr. Turman envisioned for the two men he hired was help in the preparation of one of his beloved practical jokes. It was only when the houseboat was disguised and on its way downstream that Mr. Turman was taken prisoner at gunpoint. At gunpoint, I say! His life placed in jeopardy by these criminal types. The boat was secreted on Red Deer Island, as we know, and Dalton was subjected to torture and mutilation." Dalton held up one hand to reveal that a finger was missing. Willey's voice dropped to a dramatic whisper. "You can see before your very eyes one of the more obvious results of that horrifying torture. They forced him to reveal where the company funds were secreted on the boat. Then, these killers, these villains, these psychopaths, turned on each other, and one was murdered by the hand of the other."

"What about those secreted funds, that's what I'm interested in?" Randy Dice yelled out as his first contribution to the meeting.

"I was going to . . ." Dalton started to say, but was silenced by Willey's wagging finger.

"Mr. Turman was in the process of moving the funds from one bank to another in order to provide protection from certain unethical creditors. Unfortunately, the cash happened to be on the boat at the time of his abduction."

"That was convenient," Norbert said.

"Mr. Turman was then held prisoner on an ancient cabin cruiser by the remaining fiend. This sociopath intended to extort additional money from Mrs. Pandora Turman at a future date, but this dastardly plan was foiled by Mr. Turman's daring escape. A formal statement will be issued by my office in three days."

"You can't do that!" Rocco bellowed.

Willey Lynch resumed his seat and laced his hands together over his stomach. "But we can and we have," he said.

"What about the insurance money we were paid?" Sam asked.

"We have already begun negotiating the details with the insurance carrier," Willey responded. "They do, of course, have a right to lien this property, but I believe that we shall convince them that their best interests lie in the continuation of the project. They will become an unwilling joint venturer in the property along with the other partners."

"I don't believe what I'm hearing," Norbert said.

Bea whispered in Lyon's ear, "My God, what did you do with Bobby?"

"I sent him on a short boat trip."

"Where, Cuba, Brazil, or wherever escaped people go?"

"Where is this bad guy now?" Rocco asked.

"We do not know," Willey said. "By now he knows of Mr. Turman's escape and has probably fled with the money."

"I say bust him and sort out the details later," Norbert said as he looked morosely into his empty glass, which was quickly refilled.

"Try it, buster," Doris Lemming said, "and I'll have your ass in triplicate."

"My sentiments exactly," Willey said with a beatific smile. "I emphasize again that you have no probable cause and that the courts will treat you severely."

"What about the escrow accounts he raped?" Sam asked.

"If I must repeat myself. Mr. Turman was in the process of moving the money from one account to another when it was stolen."

"I can sum this all up in one word," Rocco said.

"Enough!" Willey said harshly. "I have briefly outlined Mr. Turman's recent tribulations, but I must inform you that against my legal advice, he has chosen not to file civil and criminal charges against all of you, your organizations, your towns, and the State of Connecticut. It is only past army associations with two men here, and his strong sense of civic duty, that preclude him from embarrassing everyone concerned in this mishandled series of events."

183

"I don't believe what I just heard," Rocco said.

"What charges?" Captain Norbert was finally able to ask.

"Possible criminal charges could be bought against Mr. and Mrs. Wentworth working in concert with Chief Herbert for theft and misuse of two valuable electronic devices. Not only was this device stolen, but it was illegally installed in the telephone at Mr. Turman's residence." Caught up in his further revelations, Willey had begun to pace again.

"Lyon is not an officer of the law," Rocco said.

"Oh, but how easily that transparent veil can be pierced, Chief Herbert. He was certainly acting under your orders. He was, sir, your agent. Then we come to Senator Wentworth's attempt to extort Pan Turman's last few dollars."

"She wanted to charge me rent," Pan said. "Fifty thousand dollars' worth."

"Your attempts to arrest Mr. Turman are a clear-cut violation of his civil rights. A federal charge, I might point out. The improper identification of the body as Mr. Turman not only caused untold anguish to his wife, but resulted in the cessation of further search efforts for the victim. A jury, in its deliberations of how much money to award for this extreme anguish, would certainly question as to why prudent autopsy procedures were not carried out. Why was there no scientific match attempted between the amputated finger and the finger joint on the cadaver?"

"The body we found had the same missing finger," Norbert said.

"But, and the jury would be pointed in this direction during my summation, no attempt at a match was made."

"Lyon told me they did that and it didn't match," Pan said.

"I have the records and I have spoken with the Medical Examiner," Willey said. "It was not done."

"You lied!" Pan screamed at Lyon.

"Would you keep her quiet," Willey said to Dalton. "Mr. Turman has temporarily forbidden me to bring these charges. However, any further harassment of my client will result in a veritable blizzard of lawsuits. Do we make ourselves clear?"

"I've done the paperwork already," Doris Lemming said, "and we have some other interesting babies waiting in the closet."

"Can they do that?" the machine gunner at the bar asked no one in particular.

Captain Norbert lurched from his chair and hurried toward the door. "I've got to talk to the prosecuting attorneys."

Pan was still agitated, and she attempted to rush toward Lyon, but was restrained by Dalton. Willey pulled her into a huddled conversation.

Lyon walked over to Randy Dice's table. "I've got to ask it again, Randy. What did Dalton say to you that day on the boat?"

"He threatened to tell the people I swing with that I had AIDS."

"Let's talk," Dalton interrupted as he guided Lyon by the arm toward the patio doors.

"Wait!" Willey called after them. When Dalton continued leading Lyon outside, the lawyer lumbered after them. "You speak with no one," he commanded.

"I'm quite capable of handling Wentworth," Dalton said.

"You will speak to no one without my presence," Willey said. "Not even in the dead of night or the height of passion will you speak with your own wife without calling me first. Those are my orders. Is that understood, Mr. Turman?"

Dalton jauntily took Lyon's arm. "I speak with whom I wish. Let us not forget who is the employer here, Mr. Lynch. Is *that* understood?"

The resentment was obvious in the lawyer's face. He looked after them a moment as if prepared to continue the confrontation, but then shrugged and returned to the ballroom. The two men continued down the winding walk to the water. The gas lamps were on and the sun had disappeared over the horizon. They stopped at the low seawall that separated the lawn from the narrow beach. Dalton ran his hands quickly over Lyon's torso.

"I'm not wired, Dalton."

"Guess not, but to be on the safe side talk directly toward the sea in case those jokers have parabolic mikes somewhere around here. You know, Willey is a whore, but he's a brilliant whore."

"Was this business with him a part of the original plan or your fallback position?"

Dalton laughed. "I'm not answering that one even hypothetically, but you have to admit that it does seem to be falling into place nicely."

"If they ever find Brumby he may not verify your story."

"If they find him. He has plenty of money, and I'm sure he's out of the country by now."

"In a certain sense, I imagine that he is," Lyon said.

Dalton looked at Lyon with a wide smile. There was a trace of arrogant superiority in the look. "Why don't you tell me how you think it all happened?"

Lyon realized that to Dalton, recognition of his cleverness was a narcotic. It was the same attitude he exhibited after the climax of an elaborate prank—others must know, others must see the results and know the instigator. It was arrogant, but it was motivated by a need stronger than the good advice his attorney offered. It was a weakness that might be used to Lyon's advantage.

"I am convinced that you fully intended for me to eventually discover the houseboat and see you hanging in the stateroom," Lyon said. "I think that you counted on my identification of your body prior to the fire. Brumby and Stockton were to take me somewhere, but certainly not kill me. When they decided to go into business for themselves, you had to change plans since you thought they had killed your eyewitness. That required the finger amputation. You knew the fire would bring activity, and they had to find something definite to identify the body as yours. One finger, a minor price to pay for a positive identification of the body. You killed Katrina Loops and hung it on Bobby because she knew too much."

Dalton shook his head. "Do you think anyone operating in such a complicated scenario would risk coming to the resort to off some bimbo? Her killing was sloppy, Lyon. Unnecessary and sloppy."

"Then Pandora killed Katrina. You could afford that risk, and she was probably more than willing."

"You know Pan, hard to drop old habits: coffee, tea, or off your mistress, sir."

"Brumby would be the weak link, and so he had to be eliminated also."

"If what you say were true, that would be the logical next step," Dalton said.

"Willey can continue his legal maneuvering for a long time, and perhaps keep you from being formally charged with anything, but I doubt that the people in Rhode Island would consider your legal and civil rights in their collection efforts."

"Well, hypothetically, if I had done all that you say, the

next thing I'd do would be to pay off the loan sharks and get them off my back."

"Exactly," Lyon said. "When I convinced Pan that we knew you were alive, you already had a strong fallback position, or was it always your intention to return?"

"It's always good to be back among friends, Lyon."

"There is one fault in your otherwise flawless structure, Dalton."

"Oh, really? I would have thought anyone clever enough to plan something so complicated would have considered every eventuality."

"Brumby's body is somewhere," Lyon said. "When we find it, and establish the time of death as the night of the houseboat fire, everything else falls apart. No kidnapping would have been possible if there were no one to have held you prisoner. Three men were on that island, and if two died on the same night . . ."

"I'd be in deep shit, wouldn't I?" Dalton said. The tight grin now seemed false. "You know, Lyon, as you were talking just now, I remembered something that happened on that old cabin cruiser where I was held prisoner. I do believe I heard Brumby on deck fooling with the anchor, and then a loud splash. We were still moving, so I don't know where he went in the drink, but if he did, tied to the anchor, well, there wouldn't be much left of him when he was found, if he were found. Beats me how they could establish a time of death within weeks, much less days."

"There's an interesting parasitical worm that lives out in that water. Its life cycle is well known and completely documented by marine biologists."

"What in the hell are you talking about, Wentworth?"

"Oh, this is just a little forensic pathology lore, Dalton. It seems that this parasite enters a dead host in larvae form, and while continuing to live in the host, grows into its various life-cycle forms. Once the host is discovered and the worm removed, it's possible to determine within days how long they have remained together. In our case, an examination of Brumby's remains and the worms it contains will tell us exactly how long the body was immersed."

"That's insane."

"A useful tool, nonetheless."

"They never found Jimmy Hoffa, Judge Crater, or Martin Bormann."

"You counted on me finding the houseboat. Don't you think I'm capable of finding the body?"

"There's a hell of a lot of water out there," Dalton said.

"And I know you quite well," Lyon retorted.

His supercilious facade dropped as Dalton closed his hand painfully over Lyon's arm. "Listen, you effete son of a bitch, you screw me on this and I'll kill you."

"I believe you," Lyon said.

16

Bea was frantic.

She stood on the patio of Nutmeg Hill looking through the telescope. She had tried kitchen chores during the early morning, but her nerves made her clumsy and ineffective, so she had come outside to wait. A small boat on the river moved slowly toward the bank below the house. She adjusted the focus until the boat operator's head was clearly defined in the lens.

It was Bobby Douglas, and she sighed in relief. He was a day late, but at least he was back. He moored at the bank and began to make his way up the steep hill toward the house. Their homestead had survived another threat.

Lyon sat morosely at his desk in the study and looked out the window. Rocco and Captain Norbert sat in the leather chairs behind him sorting impatiently through their files on the Turman case.

"I'm not getting any cooperation from the feds or the state," Norbert complained. "I even had the major make a personal call to the Attorney General, and I still can't get a warrant on the bastard."

"I don't think they want to tangle with Willey Lynch if they can avoid it," Rocco said.

"Bunch of goddamn pussy cats," Norbert said as he slammed his briefcase shut and snapped the locks.

Bobby was still climbing the hill and did not respond to Bea's wave. She climbed atop the parapet and windmilled both arms. He saw her frantic movements and waved back. "Where were you last night?" she yelled.

"Over at Orient Point," he called back.

"That's across the Sound on Long Island. You're not supposed to leave the state."

"I got a lady friend over there," Bobby said through cupped hands as he approached the cusp of the promontory.

"You violated the terms of your bail for sex?" Bea called down to him.

"Lady, I been in jail."

Lyon, all too aware of the two senior police officers right behind him, moaned as his head sank down on the word processor.

"Tell them damn seagulls screeching out there to be quiet," Rocco said.

"I didn't hear a damn word about any seagull going out of state," Norbert said.

"Brumby's body is somewhere in the Sound," Lyon said as he swiveled his chair to face them. "If we find it and can establish the time of death within forty-eight hours, we've got Dalton. His statement does not allow for any alternative except that Brumby had to live days past the fire on the island."

"We don't know for sure that he dumped the body in the water," Norbert said.

"He probably did," Rocco said. "He only had a small skiff, and why bother to bring it ashore for burial when he had miles of water to deep-six it in?"

"Sure," Norbert said. "Miles of water which includes the whole of Long Island Sound, part of the Atlantic Ocean, and dozens of inlets, rivers, and harbors. We'll never find that body unless it breaks loose and becomes a floater. I'm getting out of here to go do something useful, like setting speed traps." He clumped from the room and slammed out the front door.

"Could they tell what started the fire on the island?" Lyon asked.

"Thermite and a timer."

"What type of clock?"

"An ordinary kitchen windup timer. Which means that the setting could have been anything from a few minutes to a maximum of an hour."

"That's interesting information," Lyon said.

"You think on it," Rocco said, "while I go home and see if I can talk my way out of the doghouse." He left the house, and Lyon heard the police cruiser's usual high acceleration down the drive.

"The prodigal has returned," Bea said as she came into the study arm in arm with Bobby Douglas. "Now can we chain him in the cellar until his trial, or perhaps wall him up in the breakfast nook?"

"Hell, Mrs. Wentworth, I wasn't tempted to take off more than five or six times. I could have made it to Kennedy Airport before you guys knew I was gone."

Bea sank into a leather chair. "Please, don't joke like that."

"Did you get the chart and depths?" Lyon asked.

"Sure did." Bobby pulled a nautical chart from his back pocket and spread it across the floor. Lyon took a protractor and magic marker from the desk and knelt on the floor at the edge of the map.

"What did you learn?" Lyon asked.

Bobby took the magic marker from Lyon and drew a wide circle around Red Deer Island. "The water right around the island is very shallow. Beyond the shoals, you get into lobster territory. There are lobster pots all over the damn place about here." He brushed a hand across a large swatch of water.

"Lobsters don't live at great depths, and the pots rest on the bottom," Lyon said. "So everything in that circle you drew is shallow water."

"There really aren't many deep depths until beyond the continental shelf, but there are some areas where the bottom drops off fast."

"The explosive's timer had a maximum setting of one hour," Lyon said. "Dalton would probably have killed Brumby and put the weighted body in the dinghy before he set the timer. He had less than an hour to reach an area away from any lobster pots that had sufficient depth for the safe disposal of the body."

"How do you calculate less than an hour?" Bea asked.

"Within an hour he not only had to dump the body overboard, but he had to reach land and get out of sight."

"A-ha," Bea said, "because once the explosion and fire started, the whole area would be crawling with police and Coast Guard boats."

"Exactly," Lyon said. "He knew his time was limited, and he couldn't run the risk of having another boat pass him while the body was still aboard, much less being stopped for questioning. We have two basic factors to consider: the maximum distance he could travel to deep water and still make landfall within an hour; and where are those areas of deep water."

"How deep is deep water?" Bobby asked.

"Over fifty feet," Lyon answered. "In anything less the body would run the risk of fishing-line snags or divers. Would Dalton have charts on the houseboat showing water depth?"

"Sure," Bobby said. "All that he'd need would be a chart, a compass to take a bearing from the island, and a good eye for distance." He looked at the chart on the floor and began to measure distances. "There's still a lot of water."

"Not so much," Lyon said. "Remember the time limitation and the low speed of that little boat."

Their calculations precluded any heading directly seaward or toward Long Island, and their plots were in tangent lines toward the shoreline. It quickly became obvious that any movement in those directions reduced the availability of deep water.

"There's really only one good spot," Bobby said as he made a circle around a depth marking on the chart. "It's got to be in this vicinity. Hell, it's not even a large area. We can do it ourselves."

"Do what ourselves?" Bea asked from the doorway.

"We have scuba gear and a depth finder on the rented runabout," Lyon said. "We can make the dive today."

"You're not a trained diver," Bea said.

"I am," Bobby said. "It'll be like hunting rubber ducks in a bathtub."

"Call the Coast Guard," she advised. "Let them do it."

"The Coast Guard would never authorize an underwater search based on our conjectures," Lyon said. "We'll make the dive, and if we locate the body, the authorities can take it from there."

"I can't believe that you have picked one spot in the

thousands of square miles of water out there, and really expect to find a corpse."

"It makes sense to me, Mrs. Wentworth," Bobby said.

"I want you to keep this confidential, Bea," Lyon said. "Not one word to anyone."

"Will she keep quiet?" Bobby asked later as they scrambled down the steep path to where the boat was moored.

"Of course not," Lyon replied. "She doesn't trust me around water more than three feet deep. She's probably on the phone to Rocco right now."

Bobby, wearing a wetsuit, stood at the midships control console, while Lyon peered at the depth finder's flickering display. They slowly circled Red Deer Island to take their compass bearing, and Lyon lined the azimuth up with a water tower a few miles away on the shore. They would have to estimate by dead reckoning the exact distance to the location they had selected, but the depth finder would pinpoint the spot once the bottom dropped off to the greater depth.

Lyon called the depth readings as they slowly headed toward the distant water tower. Eighteen . . . fifteen . . . Mark Twain . . ."

"Huh?" Bobby looked over at him with a puzzled glance.

"That's twelve feet," Lyon said as he decided not to offer any detailed explanation of archaic Mississippi riverboat soundings.

"We should be nearly there," Bobby said.

"I think the bottom is dropping off now," Lyon answered.

"I'm beginning to wonder, Mr. Wentworth. He might not have been this careful and just dumped the body anywhere."

"Dalton is always careful. He prides himself in thinking things completely through. He knows that the Sound is getting as crowded as the Long Island Expressway. Scuba divers, fishers, people dropping anchors right and left. I don't think he'd risk an easy discovery. Hold it!"

Bobby immediately put the engine into neutral and the boat began to slowly drift. "You have it?"

Lyon called off the readings. "Forty feet, sixty-two, seventy, ninety-three. Ninety-two. This is it."

"Okay." Bobby threw a sea anchor overboard and began to pull on the air tank straps. Lyon helped him with the equipment. "Hand me the flippers, and I'll need the belt weights."

"Now, remember," Lyon said. "If you find the body, don't touch it. We'll mark the location with a buoy."

"I'm not about to touch it." He finished donning the equipment, adjusted the face mask, and inserted the mouthpiece. He gave Lyon a thumbs-up signal and tumbled backward off the boat and quickly sank out of sight.

Lyon leaned far out over the side to watch the diver's progress. He estimated Bobby's depth to be between twenty to thirty feet when the lamp switched on. The dim glow gave the dark, sinking figure a surrealistic appearance. The light shrank in size and brilliance as the diver's descent continued, until all that could be seen was a small glow deep in the dark waters of the Sound. He leaned back in the boat. All that he could do now was wait. A small coastal freighter moved slowly across the horizon, and a sailboat running before the wind was several miles away. The distant shore was a haze as the day darkened. The clouds were taking on an ominous look, and the waves were cresting in whitecaps as the motorboat pitched alarmingly in the rising sea. Spray began to whip his face. A storm was approaching, and he wondered if small-craft warnings had been posted.

Bobby erupted from the water and grasped the gunnel with both hands. He removed the mouthpiece and pushed the mask up on his forehead. "I need another tank, this one is getting low."

"Look at the sky," Lyon said as he gestured toward the darkening clouds. "We had better head in."

"One more dive. I'm into it now, and tomorrow we'd have to start all over again."

Lyon saw his determination, and he helped him replace the used air tank with a fresh one. Bobby adjusted his equipment and sank back under the water.

A "V" of white foam broke before the prow of the long speedboat careening toward Lyon. It made broad sweeping maneuvers as it tore toward him at full speed. It swept by fifty yards away, and its wake nearly broached his boat. The boat operator's facial features were indistinct due to his foul-weather gear, but he glanced in Lyon's direction as he put the craft into a tight turn.

"Damn drunken boaters," Lyon mumbled aloud as he turned his attention back to the air bubbles breaking to the surface next to the boat. The approaching engine roar registered subliminally at first, but he turned as the sound steadily increased in volume. The powerful speedboat was heading directly toward him.

"Hey!" Lyon yelled. "Watch it!" The other craft was on a direct collision course. He knew the operator saw him, but he not only didn't change course, he seemed to slightly correct his approach to aim more directly at the middle of Lyon's boat. It was too late for any course change to matter. They were going to collide.

Lyon dove over the stern transom.

The cigarette boat's size and momentum carried it directly across the smaller boat without slowing its speed. The splintering crunch of the collision sprayed pieces of debris and Lyon instinctively ducked underwater. When he surfaced, there was no trace remaining of his boat. A hundred yards away, the cigarette boat was again making another turn.

Its operator had reduced speed and seemed to be correcting his trajectory to aim directly at him. If he was not killed by the knife-edged prow of the boat, the powerful inboard engines would suck him toward their blades and cut him to pieces.

He began to swim with the knowledge that the oncoming boat could easily compensate for his slow movements and kill him.

The pressure on his right ankle was firm and unrelenting. He tried to kick free, but the grip on his foot tightened. His forward momentum was lost as his body was pulled deeper into the water until he was standing upright. He flailed his arms to keep afloat. The speedboat would momentarily be upon him.

Lyon took a last deep breath as the pull on his lower body was more than his arms could counteract. His head slipped underwater as he was dragged down.

Bobby Douglas was killing him.

His theories were incorrect. His carefully constructed scenario of the crimes was wrong. Bobby and Dalton were still partners. Dalton, on the surface in the powerful boat, was attacking him in one way, while his cohort below was lethal in another.

His breath was gone. In seconds he would involuntarily gasp and drowning would be almost immediate.

Bobby's face was parallel to his. The diver's hands cupped his head as he brought his masked face closer to Lyon's. One hand slowly removed the mouthpiece. Air bubbles escaped into the water and churned toward the surface as Bobby pushed the mouthpiece into Lyon's mouth.

Lyon took a deep breath. Cool oxygen filled his lungs

and the panic began to subside. He pushed the mouth-piece back to Bobby.

The dark hull on the surface above them continued making circles over their location. They could feel the rush of agitated water from the boat's powerful engines as they shared the oxygen from the tank on Bobby's back.

They continued their strange, limbolike submerged floating as they shared oxygen and waited.

11 They broke to the surface together. Both men gasped and drew great gulps of air into their lungs. Bobby shucked off the harness of the empty oxygen tank while Lyon kicked off his shoes. They tred water momentarily to orient themselves in the rising swells. "Over that way." Lyon pointed toward a blinking red aircraft warning light on the distant water tower.

"I found him down there," Bobby said. "I don't know if it's the guy you're looking for, but there's a man on the bottom whose feet are wired to cement blocks."

"Good work," Lyon said. "Now, let's go home." They began to swim toward the shore in long, easy strokes that conserved as much energy as possible. Bobby, protected from the cool water by the wetsuit and swimming more efficiently because of the flippers, tended to pull ahead. He would slow and wait for Lyon to pull abreast before continuing.

"It'll be easier if you use the flippers. I've played enough tennis to be able to swim forever," Bobby said before the top of his head exploded.

Bobby Douglas slipped underwater surrounded by a widening pool of red. Another burst from the automatic rifle tripped across the surface spewing small geysers that passed inches away from Lyon.

A thickening surface mist had kept them from seeing the silent motorboat as it drifted nearby. Dalton stood in the stern with the assault rifle as he jammed a fresh magazine into the weapon. The boat began to drift closer as Lyon tred water. Dalton worked a live round into the chamber and waited for the distance to close even further. "Find it, Lyon?" he called.

"He's down there."

Dalton's laugh was the same as it had always been. "Too bad." He slowly brought the assault rifle to his shoulder and took careful aim.

The Coast Guard cutter that curved out of the mist had the familiar vertical red stripe near its bow, and a crewman on the forward deck manned a .50-caliber machine gun. "We are going to board you," an official voice announced over the cutter's loud-speaker system.

As Dalton automatically turned to look at the cutter, Lyon dove. His hands clutched for water as he pulled himself deeper and deeper underwater. The Klasnikov clattered above him. Bullets churned the water by his side but passed harmlessly.

Lyon felt the vibrations of the speedboat's powerful engines as the dark shape above him began to move rapidly away.

His head popped out of the water and he found himself framed in a circle of light from the cutter's searchlight. Two frogmen plunged from the deck. They landed with a splash in the penumbra of the light. One sailor stroked toward Lyon, the other toward Bobby Douglas, who floated ten yards to the right.

The diver encircled Lyon's body below the shoulders with the flotation device and then looked at his face. "Jeez! I know you. I pulled you out of the water a couple of days ago."

Lyon nodded. "Thanks again."

"It's a drill," the diver yelled over to his companion. "This guy's a plant 'cause I pulled him out a couple of days ago. It's only a drill."

"Drill, hell, you dork," the other frogman yelled. "My guy's head is missing."

Lyon was winched up to the deck of the cutter where Rocco Herbert waited. "The captain says no one is dumb enough to fall in twice in a row. I told him he didn't know you."

Lyon pointed to the body that was slowly being pulled aboard. "Dalton killed him."

"Was that Douglas?"

"Yes. Can we please go get Dalton?"

When the frogmen were aboard, the cutter began to move in the direction of the motorboat, which was barely visible in the distance. "He's going for the resort," Rocco yelled over the loud throb of the ship's engines. "He's a lot faster than we are, but Norbie's already out there with a bunch of his guys."

They watched silently as two crewmen carefully placed Bobby's body in a rubber body bag and zippered it shut. After the corpse was stowed below, Rocco and Lyon worked their way to the bow. The cutter heeled at a jaunty angle as it ran at full speed, but it was still unable to close the distance between them and the rapidly moving cigarette boat. Rocco raised his binoculars as they rounded the point for the final approach to the resort. Dalton was still far ahead and on a direct heading for the resort's small beach. Rocco handed the glasses to Lyon with a single comment. "Look."

Pan was running down the walk from her cottage. She waved her arms frantically at the approaching boat. Her mouth was open in what to them was a silent scream. Troopers poured from the main building at the top of the walk and began to rush in a skirmisher's line toward the beach.

Dalton veered his boat until it ran parallel to the resort beach a few yards from shore. They heard the distant chug of his automatic weapon, and Pan's forward momentum froze as she crumpled over the seawall in a rag-doll flail of limbs.

"Even Willey Lynch won't get him out of that one," Rocco said as Dalton's boat swerved around the point toward open water.

The sailor at the mounted .50-caliber machine gun behind them rearmed his weapon. He swiveled it in the direction of Dalton. "I can waste that sucker!" he yelled.

Rocco pushed the weapon barrel aside. "The bastard's not getting away. We'll get him."

The cutter changed the direction of its pursuit as its dual searchlights crisscrossed each other in an attempt to frame the speedboat in their beams. "Where in the hell is he going?" the sailor behind them yelled.

"Toward the mouth of the Connecticut River," Rocco said. "He knows we can bracket him in the open sea, his only chance is to land and run for it."

"Doesn't Middleburg have a police boat?" Lyon asked.

"Sure does," Rocco said.

"Why don't you radio ahead and have them start on their way downstream?"

"Damn good idea." Rocco hurried to the bridge. He was back in minutes. "The Middleburg boat is on its way, and the state police helicopter also. We're going to corner the bastard."

They were nearly to Murphysville when they saw the lights of the Middleburg boat as it made its way downriver. The police helicopter made its first pass over the escaping boat and the distance between the three vessels began to narrow as Dalton was forced to throttle back.

An icy knot began to form in Lyon's stomach. He had a vast sense of impending doom as he calculated Dalton's next probable move. He could only hope that Bea, out of a sense of immense curiosity, was either on the patio or at one of the windows so that she could see what was transpiring on the river and take actions to protect herself.

Dalton turned his boat directly toward the shore below Nutmeg Hill promontory and ran it aground. He began to make his way up the steep hill toward the house and Bea.

"Take him out!" Rocco roared at the sailor at the mounted machine gun.

"He's behind rocks, I can't get a clear shot!"

Bea sat in the breakfast nook with half a cup of cold coffee in front of her and a yellow legal pad. Several crumpled sheets of paper were on the floor by her side. She had listed all the state senators on the page for the seventh time and had neatly placed her yea and nay tallies by each name. No matter how she calculated, her daycare amendment could pass, but there were not enough votes to override the Governor's veto. She took a sip of coffee and grimaced at its taste. She walked into the kitchen and poured fresh coffee from the electric per-colator.

She saw out the double windows over the sink that there was activity on the river. A launch was moving from a Coast Guard cutter in the main channel toward the shore below the house. She smiled. That's good service, she thought. They were delivering the three men right to the doorstep, so to speak. She would write a very nice note to the commandant.

The kitchen door behind her opened and she turned with a smile. "Home is the hunter, home . . ." Dalton Tur-man stood in the door pointing an automatic rifle directly at her.

"Hi, honey," he said. "How would you like a vacation?"

She knew instantly that Lyon had discovered what he was looking for, that Dalton knew it, and that the men landing at the base of the hill were after him. Her smile didn't fade. "Stop pointing that damn thing at me, Dalton. You're getting so that you aren't funny anymore."

He pushed her aside to look out the window. "Don't play cute, Bea. You know why Lyon was out on the Sound today."

"Did he find the body?"

"He said he did. They were at the right location."

"Lyon's very good at putting things like that together," she said.

He turned away from the window. "Yes, isn't he."

"It won't take them long to get up the hill, Dalton. The car keys are on the pegboard in the corner. The car's in the drive and I filled the tank with gas earlier today."

"I really appreciate your cooperation and concern, Bea-trice," Dalton said. "But what we have here now is what's called your basic hostage situation. You know that Rocco must have talked to his men by radio. I wouldn't get past the drive."

"Oh, come on now, Dalton. You know these things never work out. No one ever gets away and Rocco wouldn't let you past the city limits if you had a busload of hostages."

Dalton pressed the barrel of his weapon against her forehead. "I am not some idiot holed up in a bank who takes two clerks hostage and tries to escape on a Greyhound. I have some variations that will blow your mind."

The phone startled both of them. "It's probably the hostage negotiators," Bea said. "This is where you demand a seven-forty-seven and a million in cash." The phone rang again.

"A small helicopter will do. Answer it."

Bea carefully pushed the gun barrel away from her forehead, but Dalton kept it pointed at her midriff. She picked up the receiver. "Yes?" She listened a moment and then covered the mouthpiece with her hand. "It's the Governor," she said to Dalton.

"I've got to hand it to Lyon, he goes to the top in no time at all. Tell the Governor I want a helicopter in ten minutes or I blow your head off."

Bea nodded and began to speak slowly and clearly into the phone. "Please listen carefully. I am a hostage . . . No! Not to my liberal beliefs. I am a hostage hostage. There is a man in my kitchen holding a Klasnikov to my head . . . No, I am not making an ethnic joke . . . There is a man holding a machine gun in my kitchen . . . I don't care what I said about gun control last session! Will you listen to me, you idiot? I am about to be killed!"

"Now Rocco and Lyon are on the line too," Bea said to Dalton.

He snatched the phone from her hand and shoved her into the corner. "This isn't party-line time! Listen out there! You have," he looked at his watch, "eight minutes for the bird to be on the field in back of the house . . .

You want a what, Wentworth? . . . An exchange? I take you in place of Bea? Fine, come on in. Make sure you come in the back way and walk in the yard spot so I can see you clearly. And strip . . . You heard me. Come in here in your underwear. Make it snappy!"

He started to slam the receiver back into its stanchion, but Bea took it from his hand. "I know you're recording this, so tell fearless leader that you'll release the transcript at my funeral if he doesn't approve my child-care amendment. Got that? Promise? . . . And for God's sake don't let Lyon come in here."

Dalton snatched the phone and pulled her around the corner into the protected confines of the hall. "You're nuts, do you know that?"

"Sometimes you have to use every available political weapon, and I have a feeling that I may not have many parliamentary alternatives in my future."

In the shadows of the tree line, Lyon began removing his clothes. Across the lawn he saw the house, now ominous and dangerous. He arranged his clothes in a neat pile by his feet and took off everything except his jockey shorts. Dalton hadn't mentioned shoes, but he took them off also.

"You can't go," Rocco said from the shadows at his side. Lyon didn't answer. "You do remember what he said to you by the seawall? He said he would kill you."

"I know," Lyon said, "and I don't believe he's going to let Bea go, but it has to be done." The spotlight mounted over the back steps cast a swatch of light that carried half-across the yard nearly to the edge of the garden shed. Once past the shed, he would be in clear view of the kitchen door and a side window. It was at that point of no return where the ring of town and State Police with their M-16s and other weapons would be of no help.

"I think we could tape a flat automatic pistol to the small of your back," Rocco said. "That's the only way you can carry any sort of weapon in there. Or maybe a combat knife? We could hide that under the waistband."

"God, Rocco, I'm not a knife fighter, and he's going to check me as soon as I'm in there. Just make sure the helicopter lands in a few minutes." Lyon broke away from Rocco's restraining grip. He stepped out from the tree line and began the walk toward the rim of light near the house.

His legs felt leaden, his feet chunky, and the longish grass seemed to grasp his toes like restraining tentacles. He had no plan, only fear that he attempted to shove deep into the corner of his mind. He had walked this path twenty thousand times, and now the familiar had turned strange. The shape of trees and the configuration of the house appeared foreign.

He was only a few feet from the storage shed. Its door had never been properly closed since the dummy incident, and the evening wind caused it to wave back and forth and clunk against the wall with a hollow sound. He thought of the electric hedge clippers. He was probably the only gardener in the state who had recently managed to cut through his own clipper cord while trimming a bush. The useless clippers with their severed electric cord still hung on a nail in the shed.

He stepped into the shed and snaked the cut cord from its hook, coiled it quickly, and stuffed it into the rear of his shorts. Within seconds he was out of the shed and walking in the circle of light near the rear of the house.

Lyon stepped into the empty kitchen. He had expected to be shot crossing the yard while clearly outlined in the light, but he now realized that Dalton's firing might have triggered an immediate police assault. He obviously had other plans. They were probably in the hall, hidden from a direct sighting by police sharpshooters. He only had seconds left before he faced the man with the assault rifle. Lyon let the kitchen door noiselessly close behind him and tore the damaged electrical cord from his shorts. He plugged the line into the socket on the kitchen counter where the percolator still operated. Its naked end dangled over the counter rim and fell halfway to the floor.

He stood in the center of the room and urinated. He felt the warm fluid trickle down his legs, over his bare toes, and form a pool around his feet. "Anybody home?" he called.

"Don't move," Dalton commanded from the hall.

Bea, with one arm bent behind her back, was shoved into the hallway door in such a manner that her shoulder touched the wall and provided a protected rest for Dalton's rifle. She tried to smile at Lyon, but her eyes were wide and there was a marked quaver to her voice. "You look ridiculous in those shorts," she said.

"You've always said that."

Only a small portion of Dalton's face was visible behind Bea, but the gun barrel on her shoulder rotated slightly until it was pointed directly at Lyon. "Raise your arms and turn around," Dalton ordered.

Lyon did as directed. "Let her go."

Dalton laughed. "You didn't really think that I would? I need both of you. One on each flank. Good God! You've wet yourself. Look at your brave husband, Bea. He just peed in his pants. Now that I think back, he did that in his foxhole in combat when I had to pull him out. Jesus, what a whimp."

Lyon sagged forward as his hands clutched at his face. "I can't stand any more. Please let us go."

"Don't, Lyon," Bea said in a faraway voice.

"I know he's going to kill us," Lyon said as his knees wobbled.

The clatter of a helicopter's approach filled the room. "As soon as it lands we go out. And you two better be all over me or none of us makes it."

"They'll follow us," Bea said.

"Wait until you see how I make a helicopter disappear," Dalton said.

Lyon sank to his knees on the kitchen floor. "He'll never let us land alive."

"I promise you a landing one way or the other," Dalton said.

"It's too much," Lyon pleaded. "Kill me now."

"And have them rush the house as soon as they hear a shot? No way," Dalton said.

"I beg you," Lyon pleaded.

"Please," Bea said to Lyon.

"You sniveling bastard!" Dalton said as he pushed past Bea. He reversed the rifle preparatory to smashing a butt stroke to Lyon's head. "You're no good to me on your knees."

"God help us," Lyon said as his right hand closed around Dalton's ankle and his left simultaneously grasped the naked end of the plugged cord.

Bea screamed as the two men's bodies arced in a macabre dance of convoluted movements as the electricity surged through them. Lyon's nearly naked body, in direct contact with the liquid on the floor, flopped convulsively for several seconds before his heart went into arrest, and still the convulsing movements continued. Dalton's fingers were locked on the trigger guard of the assault rifle, and as they jerked, the weapon fired and sent half a magazine of bullets through his torso, and barely missed Bea as she flung herself into the hallway in her scrambled clawing for the circuit breaker box.

Bea stood on the patio at the parapet as she looked out over the river valley with unseeing eyes. She felt a grief too profound for tears, too intense for any immediate emotion other than a numb realization of what had just happened. She was aware that blood spatters pocked her clothes, arms, and face. It was the stigma of the final gift of the final prank of the man whose greed had destroyed so many. There was nothing she could do. Anything that could be done, would be done, by the large man struggling with the dead in the crowded kitchen.

Rocco's anguished cry of "No!" caused her to turn and look through the kitchen window. The large police chief held the medic with the body bag by the front of his shirt. "Out!" he yelled, and threw the man through the kitchen door.

She gave a stifled giggle in a display of inapproporiate emotion far removed from the horror of her reality. It would have been better if Rocco had opened the screen before he threw the medic out the door. The kitchen now had a broken door, snake-shot bullet holes in the cabinets, machine-gun bullet holes throughout the hall, blood everywhere, and a scorched floor. It didn't matter. The new owners could do the repairs, for she would never spend another night in the house that had murdered her husband.

"O Two, asshole," Rocco bellowed inside the kitchen.

That has a certain cadence to it, Bea thought before the significance of what she had just heard caused her to rush to the hall and peer into the kitchen. Rocco rose from his CPR position at Lyon's nearly naked body. An oxygen mask was attached to her husband's face. A monitor sat on the kitchen counter with its leads running to Lyon.

Numbers flickered on the monitor. "We got him!" the EMT yelled.

Bea crumpled to the floor.

The Wobblies had grown gargantuan in size and clung to the exterior of the Empire State Building. Their eyes blazed in anger as their long tails flicked dangerously to and fro. A dozen helicopters buzzed around the building and took turns in their diving attacks against the rampaging monsters. The Wobblies' tails struck again and again as they crushed flying machines and knocked them from the sky.

Lyon rooted for the monsters and kept a running tally of their destructive score. Somewhere in the distance a pinball machine pinged with metronome regularity at each monster victory. Bea was huddled on a balcony, but he knew she was well protected by the benign monsters.

A brilliant flash of light briefly illuminated the whole scene, and then it was gone. He forced his eyes open to look into the face of the towheaded resident bent over him with a penlight in his hand.

"He's coming around," the doctor said as he straightened up.

It took a few more moments for Lyon's eyes to focus and for his surroundings to merge into coherent shapes. Bea and Rocco stood at the foot of the bed, and beyond them he could see a glass window and a nurse at a monitoring station. Banks of instrumentation seemed to surround him with wire leads connected to his body. He knew he was in an intensive-care unit.

"Do you have a guard on Dalton?" Lyon asked.

Bea took his hand and squeezed. "It's not necessary."

"Didn't make it. Too bad," Lyon said. "Saved my life once. I ever tell you that?"

"Once or twice," Bea said.

"You know, Lyon," Rocco began, "it's about time we cleared that little matter up. With Dalton gone, I am released from my oath and can tell you the truth. There wasn't really a firefight that night at our perimeter. Dalton planted those army fire crackers they use for training in front of your position. When he set them off, it sounded exactly like a mortar attack. Then he pretended to come to your rescue, but it was all a put-up job, a trick, one of his pranks. You know how he was."

The drugs they had administered were making Lyon inordinately sleepy. "Thanks, Rocco, and I'll pretend that I believe that." His eyes closed. "But how was Dalton going to make the helicopter disappear?" He was very sleepy, but he would think about it, and maybe the Wobblies would know.